T0156576

HUNTER:
BOOK OF REVELATIONS

By

ART WIEDERHOLD

Order this book online at www.trafford.com
or email orders@trafford.com

Most Trafford titles are also available at major online book retailers.

© Copyright 2011 Art Wiederhold.
All rights reserved. No part of this publication may be reproduced, stored in a retrieval
system, or transmitted, in any form or by any means, electronic, mechanical, photocopying,
recording, or otherwise, without the written prior permission of the author.

Printed in the United States of America.

ISBN: 978-1-4269-8967-4 (sc)
ISBN: 978-1-4269-8968-1 (e)

Trafford rev. 08/04/2011

 www.trafford.com

North America & international
toll-free: 1 888 232 4444 (USA & Canada)
phone: 250 383 6864 ✦ fax: 812 355 4082

CHAPTER ONE:
A Rag, a Bone and a Hank of Hair

Leander Barnes was a dirty, sneaky little bastard. His greasy dark hair was stringy and unkempt and his eyes had a sinister and shifty cast to them. His lips were thick and he had gone unshaven for several days. Everything about him literally screamed that he was untrustworthy.

A real slimeball.

One of the lowest of the city's bottom feeding criminals.

It was just after midnight on a hot, summer night when Barnes entered his shabby little shotgun shack on Poydras. He used the back door so no one could see him or the large bundle he carried on his shoulder. As he entered his dingy bedroom, he tossed the bundle on top of his bed and smiled as the contents struggled.

Thinking he was safe, he switched on the light and nearly jumped out of his skin when he saw the woman in the black cloak standing next to his open window.

"What are *you* doing here?" Barnes demanded nervously, afraid that his dirty little secret had gotten out.

"I've come for *you*," the woman said as she stepped toward him.

"Me? What do ya want with me?" he piped as he stepped back.

"This!" she said as she opened her mouth and bared her fangs.

Barnes tried to run, but the woman seized his collar, lifted him off his feet and hurled him across the room. He crashed into a large oak dresser with an ornate mirror attached to it. The impact knocked several objects from the top of the dresser and shattered the mirror.

Barnes rolled off and hit then floor.

"Leaving so soon?" the woman asked. "That's bad manners!"

Before he could regain his feet, the woman grabbed him by the front of his shirt and pinned him against a wall. Then she smiled and sank her fangs into his neck.

Barnes twitched a few times, and then went still as she drained him of every last drop of blood. When she was satisfied, she let his lifeless body drop to the floor and turned her attention to the moving bundle on the bed.

There were muffled cries coming from within it.

She studied the large woolen blanket. It was bound by several heavy cords. She easily snapped each of the cords and unrolled the blanket. A small, very frightened little girl with bright red hair and green eyes stared back at her. There was gag over her mouth and her wrists and ankles were bound by the same type of cords that were around the blanket.

The woman broke the cords and removed the gag.

The child sobbed and hugged her tightly.

"That's alright, child," she said as she stroked her hair. "You're safe now. The evil man who took you is dead. He can't hurt you anymore."

She took the girl, who was just five years old, back to her frantic parents in the French Quarter. After accepting their tearful thank yous, she walked over to the police station on Basin Street to inform Inspector Leon Valmonde that Leander Barnes was no more and where he could find his body.

"I'm glad you showed up in time to save the little girl. There's no tellin' what that fiend would have done with her," Valmonde said.

He reached into his desk drawer, picked up a white envelope stuffed with bills and handed it to her.

"Thank you, Lorena. You've done the city of New Orleans a great service," he said.

Lorena smiled and left the station.

"I'm sure glad she's on our side," Valmonde said as he walked to the counter and poured himself a cup of coffee.

Lorena Concetta La Bouvier was tall and uncommonly beautiful. She had red-gold hair and deep green eyes and a smile that made most men's' knees buckle.

She was also a vampire.

While many of her kind looked upon humans as a source of food, Lorena and her lover, Hunter, tracked down and killed those who preyed on humans. They also hunted and killed other nasty creatures, like werewolves and demons. To satisfy her own hunger for human blood, Lorena preyed upon dangerous, wanted criminals like Barnes.

That's why Valmonde saw her as a friend and ally. Thanks to her, Hunter and their friends Jean-Paul DuCassal and Hannah Morii, the streets of New Orleans were now much safer.

And Valmonde had no qualms about giving Lorena the posted rewards for the criminals she rid the city of. Barnes had been one of the city's worst offenders. His head netted Lorena 5,000 Louisiana Dollars. That made it one of the largest bounties she had ever collected.

As she entered the mansion she shared with Hunter in the Garden District, she tossed the envelope on the side table next to the window and headed upstairs to the master bedroom.

Hunter was still asleep when she arrived.

And she could see that it was a fitful slumber at best.

He was having another of his frequent nightmares and he tossed and turned as images of a heated battle around a flaming village below a dark, foreboding keep raced through his subconscious.

He saw hordes of men in armor on horseback galloping to and fro, skewering people with lances or lopping off heads with swords and axes. The images came in rapid succession but seemed to have no particular order.

In the midst of the chaos, the all-too-familiar face of Baron Georgi Konstantino Vlastrada, the vampire lord who was Hunter's worst nemesis, appeared.

"Who are you?" he demanded.

Then the image faded and the flaming numerals 1462 appeared.

Hunter woke with a start. He sat up and looked at Lorena. She smiled.

"How'd it go tonight?" he asked as he ran his fingers through his hair.

"I'm no longer hungry," she replied.

He nodded and got up to dress. She sat on the bed and watched. When he was through, he turned to her.

"I have to go out," he said.

"I know," she said.

He always went for long walks after one of his nightmares. Usually, he walked over to the French Quarter and up to St. Ann Street. And on many of his walks, he encountered the spirit of Madame Marie Laveau, the most powerful voodoo queen in the history of the Crescent City.

And on each of these occasions, Lorena gave him a five minute head start then followed after him to guard his back.

Just in case.

As Hunter stepped out of the house, he saw DuCassal walking toward him. As usual, he was dressed for the hunt in his wide brimmed black hat, long canvass duster, black shirt, trousers and boots and he had his double-barreled shotgun in the crook of his arm.

He smiled.

"Mind if I join you, Charles?" he asked as he fell into step with Hunter.

Charles is what DuCassal normally called Hunter. It was the name he knew him by when they were friends during the First Age. He didn't know Hunter's surname.

Neither did Hunter.

In fact, Hunter was what one of the Cardinals at the Vatican had christened him centuries before. Hunter had no idea what his actual name was or where he came from. But he felt that the answers to both questions—and many more—lay hidden in his nightmares.

And he wasn't sure he wanted to know them.

"Rougarou or vampire?" Hunter asked.

"Rougarou. One has been sighted near Lafayette Cemetery about an hour ago. I thought we'd go search for him," DuCassal replied.

Rougarous were a type of werewolf that was prevalent to Louisiana. They could change from human to rougarou and vice-verse at will and were faster, stronger and more cunning than their European cousins.

"Where's Lorena?" asked DuCassal.

"Right here," she said as she caught up to them.

Hunter smiled.

"Let's go bag us a rougarou," he said.

After one of his nightmares, Hunter usually walked the streets of the city to shake it off. Tonight was different. With a rougarou on the prowl, he had no time to think about the dream. The beast had already killed two people. They had to find it before it could kill anyone else.

Lafayette Cemetery was a couple of blocks away. It was surrounded by a high granite wall and had two wrought iron gates for entrances. It was one of the better kept cemeteries in the city, which had 44 in all. Most dated back to the late 1700s of the First Age. Most of these "cities of the dead" featured often elaborate above ground vaults or tombs, many of which remained in use by the families who built them centuries earlier.

As they approached the cemetery, Lorena held up her hand. They stopped and looked where she nodded.

"What did you see?" asked Hunter.

"Something dark was moving among the vaults a few yards beyond the gate. It might be our rougarou," she said.

"Let's go in. Be careful and watch for an ambush," Hunter said.

They stopped just inside the gate and looked around. Seeing nothing, they walked along the main path until they came to huge orphan's monument in the middle of the cemetery. The monument was the largest in Lafayette and contained nearly 200 vaults.

They stopped there and looked carefully in all directions.

"I think I see him, mes amis. There's something lurking in the shadows at the end of that path," DuCassal said as he pointed at group of vaults about 100 yards to the right.

"Let's have a look," Hunter said as he drew his revolver.

"I'll go left," Lorena said as she disappeared into the shadows.

"I'll go right," DuCassal said as he took off.

Hunter waited and watched the shadows between the vaults, then walked straight ahead. That's when he spotted a pair of deep red eyes glaring balefully at him from the shadows between two tombs.

"I see you now. Come out and face me—if you have the balls," he challenged.

The rougarou obliged.

He stepped into the moonlight, growled and bared his fangs as he beat his chest to show he accepted Hunter's challenge.

Hunter took aim and fired.

The rougarou flinched and the shot took off his right ear. Hunter fired again. This time, the shot struck the creature in the right shoulder. The impact spun him around and elicited a cry of pain and anger from him. Realizing he was out of his league, the rougarou turned and bounded over several tombs. He hit the ground on the other side and leaped over the wall just before Hunter could catch up with him. Hunter climbed to the top of the wall and watched as the beast ran down Washington toward St. Charles.

Lorena and DuCassal caught up with Hunter just as he reached the main gate.

"Where'd it go?" asked Lorena.

"When I last saw him, he was headed for the French Quarter," Hunter replied. "Let's go after him before he kills anyone else."

They caught sight of the rougarou on Fulton Street and gave chase. The creature darted up and down several streets and between buildings until they lost sight of him near Clinton Street.

Hunter stopped and looked around. There was no sign of their quarry.

"Let's fan out so we can cover more ground. If you see him, take him down," he said.

The rougarou loped down North Front Street and turned the corner. Thinking he had eluded his pursuers, he took a deep breath and tried to relax.

"Looking for me?" said a voice that came from behind him.

The rougarou whirled around and squinted at the tall, lean man leaning against a door in a nearby building. The man wore a flat topped, wide-brimmed black hat and black opera cape with a dark red lining draped over a white, ruffled shirt. But the most striking thing about him was the stark white opera mask that covered only half his face.

The rougarou snarled and pounded his chest. The man simply remained calm and continued to puff on his thin cigar.

"Either attack me or leave. It makes little difference to me," the man said with a yawn.

Enraged by the obvious display of indifference, the rougarou bared his teeth and sprang at the man. To his horror and total disbelief, the man suddenly seized him by the throat in mid-leap then slammed him to the pavement with enough force to shatter several bricks. Before the rougarou could do another thing, his adversary suddenly morphed into a larger, stronger version of a rougarou and sunk its long, white teeth into his neck. It happened so fast that the rougarou could barely emit a gargle as the blood left its body.

By the time Hunter, Lorena and DuCassal reached the scene, their prey had already been dispatched and the tall, lean, dramatically garbed man was standing next to it wiping blood from his lips with a handkerchief. He smiled and bowed his head as they approached.

Hunter laughed.

"Good evening, Alejandro" he said as they shook hands. "I see you've bagged him for us. Thanks."

"Good evening, my friends. I hope I did not spoil your hunt," Alejandro apologized. "But this one ran right into my arms."

"Not at all. In fact, we almost lost his trail," DuCassal said as they watched the rougarou change slowly back into his human form.

"I was on my way to the Dragon for an evening meal, but this one proved to be most satisfying," Alejandro said as they walked down the street. "His blood was quite bitter. I must wash it down with a few strong, cold drinks. Would you care to join me?"

DuCassal looked back at the slain rougarou.

"He looks familiar. I think I've seen him at the Dragon once or twice," he said.

"That makes sense. Both his victims were wanna-bes from the club. That must have been his hunting ground," Hunter said.

"Unfortunately for him, he attempted to cross *my* hunting ground," Alejandro said as they headed for Bourbon Street.

Gideon Lamar Alexander, or Alex or Alejandro as he liked to be called, was due to a strange set of circumstances, a hybrid. He was part vampire and part rougarou and had a flair for the dramatic.

The half-mask also concealed the part of his face that had been badly scarred when he was caught in a fire at the age of 12. He also wore the mask because it gave a sort of "Phantom of the Opera" look.

He also enjoyed preying upon other rougarous. His unique blend made him faster, stronger and more deadly than they were. They also knew he was out there looking for them. They just didn't know who he was or where he'd turn up.

Even if they did, none of them dared take Alejandro on face-to-face. Those who tried ended up dead and bloodless in the dirty New Orleans streets.

Hunting and killing rougarous satisfied both his cravings for flesh and thirst for blood. He also preferred to keep his activities as quiet as possible. Only a handful of people knew who and what he was. As long as he only killed rougarous and left the general population alone, neither Hunter nor the police had a quarrel with him.

New Orleans was crawling with all sorts of supernatural predators and other things that refused to stay dead and buried. Anyone who helped keep them under control was doing the community a great service.

Hunter, DuCassal and Lorena considered him an ally, even if he was sort of an overly dramatic flake.

Alejandro also liked to run with the city's elite and powerful. He was independently wealthy and enjoyed flaunting it although no one knew the source of his seemingly endless supply of cash.

The fourth member of their group was Hannah Morii. She was the last in a long line of samurai and, thanks to her father's training, was an expert in several forms of martial arts. She owned the large trading company called Treasures of the Pacific on Royal and often supplied Hunter with some Asian weaponry—like his katana.

When she wasn't running the shop, Hannah was out hunting vampires. Unlike Hunter and his team, she was completely mortal and could actually be seriously wounded and even killed by the things she hunted.

Her battle against a pack of wolves at Longue Vue weeks earlier had left her badly scratched and bruised for days. She realized then that she needed an edge, something that would enable her to survive such encounters and make her a more proficient Slayer.

It was something she had discussed at great length with Lorena several times. Each time, Lorena advised her to think about it as the change she wanted would be quite permanent. After much consideration, Hannah again asked Lorena to help her.

At three p.m. the following afternoon, Lorena entered the shop and saw Hannah Morii seated behind the main counter as usual. Hannah smiled when she walked over.

"I'm glad you've come," she said.

"Are you sure you want to do this?" Lorena asked. "Do you understand what will happen to you?"

"Yes. I've given it a lot of thought. If I am to continue on my chosen path, this is the best way to assure that I'll be able to survive. This will make me more effective," Hannah replied.

"As long as you are doing this of your own free will," Lorena said.

"I am," Hannah assured her. "When can we start?"

"Now, if you like," Lorena said.

"Will it hurt?" Hannah asked as they walked into the back office and up the stairs to Hannah's apartment.

"No. It will be little more than a pinprick followed by an erotic rush," Lorena said as she removed her cloak and lay across the back of a chair. "I've never done this before. You will be my very first."

"You said I feel an erotic rush?" Hannah asked.

"Yes. Women seem to become quite aroused when bitten by a vampire. I remember feeling extremely aroused when I was turned," Lorena explained. "*Sexually aroused.*"

"What about you? Will you also become aroused?" Hannah asked.

"I don't know. I have never attempted to turn anyone before," Lorena said. "If anything happens, try not get embarrassed by your feelings."

Hannah nodded.

She undid her blouse and pulled it off. Then she lay down on the bed.

"I'm ready," she said.

Lorena removed her cloak and got in next to her. Then she gently stroked her hair and whispered softly.

"Try to relax. Don't think about what I'm doing. Just close your eyes and let your emotions flow freely," she said.

Hannah took a deep breath, closed her eyes and slowly exhaled. Lorena gently turned her head so she could get at her neck. She licked her lips, then opened her mouth and sunk her fangs into her.

Hannah gasped, and then sighed as the euphoric rush hit her. It felt more like Lorena was kissing her than anything else. After a few seconds, she began to enjoy the erotic sensations that surged through her. Lorena drank for a good two minutes, and then retracted her fangs. She sat up and smiled at Hannah.

Hannah saw the lines of blood on Lorena's chin. She reached up and touched the side of her neck. She was able to feel the bite marks.

"That felt nice," she said as she sat up. "Exciting!"

"You'll probably have to sleep for a few hours now. Probably by the fifth time, you'll have to wear dark glasses whenever you travel during the day. After the seventh, you'll sleep for three days and nights. When you wake up, you'll be just like me," Lorena explained. "If you decide to stop before the last session, you'll revert to normal in a month or two. Until then, you'll feel as if you have the flu."

Hannah dressed and smiled at her.

"The rush seems to be subsiding already. That's too bad. I was enjoying it," she said. "You're right about becoming aroused. If it had been any stronger, I would have tried to have sex with you. How did you feel? Are you aroused?"

"A little," Lorena admitted with a smile.

"Enough to where you want to have sex with me?" Hannah teased.

Lorena nodded

"Thanks, Lorena," Hannah said.

"Don't thank me yet. After the transformation is complete, you may hate me for doing this to you, especially when you get the *hunger*. You'll try to resist it at first, but eventually, you'll have to give in. You'll need human blood to survive. There's no way around that. How much you'll need depends entirely on you," Lorena said. "Just don't feed on any good people."

Hannah laughed.

"I won't. I promise," she said. "When's the next session?"

"Tomorrow afternoon. We have to do this for seven consecutive days in order for me to turn you," Lorena said as they headed back down to the shop. "Once you realize what you'll be able to do, you'll really enjoy the changes. But you're enemies won't!"

Hannah smiled and showed her out.

"I'll see you again tomorrow," she said.

That's when Hannah began to feel very drowsy. She decided to close the shop for the rest of the day and headed back upstairs to get some sleep.

When Lorena got home, she saw Hunter sitting on the porch reading the newspaper. She sat down at the table with him. He smiled.

"Did she go through with it?" he asked.

"In seven more days, a new vampire will be walking the streets of New Orleans," Lorena said. "I hope she can handle the changes."

"I'm sure she will. Hannah is very strong and determined. If she becomes as good as you are, then I pity whoever goes up against her," Hunter said. "At least I won't have to worry about her when we get into a fight."

Lorena nodded.

"I was actually afraid she would get herself killed when we fought Van Helsing. It's a miracle she survived those wolves," she said.

"That's more a testament of her martial skills than divine intervention," Hunter said. "She's very good at what she does. In fact, she's better than most I've seen, especially with that katana."

"Is she as good as you?" Lorena asked.

Hunter shrugged.

"I'd hate to have to find out," he said.

While things were going as they normally did for the people of New Orleans, life for the inhabitants of a city just 100 miles to the north had taken a decidedly ugly turn.

Baton Rouge, or Red Stick as the locals called it, was the second largest city in Louisiana. For much of the First Age, it served as the capital. Like New Orleans. Baton Rouge had also had its share of tragedies, both natural and man made. During its history, it had been totally destroyed five times.

And each time, the stubborn inhabitants had rebuilt it.

Today, it was home to about 45,000 people, most of whom scratched a living from the swamps and sugar cane plantations. Like most large towns in Louisiana, it was a mix of fine restaurants, rowdy bars, strip clubs and churches. Red Stick had a "mayor" named Bob Pell and a sheriff named Big Jim Gerber. Both were of Cajun stock and had been running things in Baton Rouge for the past 18 years.

Mostly, it was Big Jim who ran things. Pell was more of an honorary mayor at best. He was very good at making long speeches, kissing babies and cutting ribbons and other such things that mayors are supposed to do. He also had to balance the city's budget, which included paying to maintain the volunteer fire department, the sheriff's department, and the streets, sewers and public places. But it was up to Big Jim to decide who got what and when.

The city was surrounded by antebellum period plantations, most of which grew cane or rice, several small villages and primeval swamps. A single lane, semi-paved "highway" connected it to New Orleans and the very ancient city of Natchez far to the north.

It was a real peaceful city.

It had live oaks lining the main streets, beautiful homes, five good schools and several very old churches, many of which had been converted to casinos.

Hardly anything real interesting ever happened there. But during this particular summer, all that was about to change.

Hattie Ann Taliafiero (she pronounced it Toliver) was rudely awakened from her deep slumber by several loud, hard knocks on her front door. Irritated, she slapped her husband, Clem, on the backside. He just grumbled and rolled over.

Hattie scowled.

"Okay, be like that! I'll check it myself!" she said in his ear.

She got out of bed and threw on her robe. She gave Clem one last dirty look, then headed downstairs to see what danged fool would come knocking in the middle of night like that. Feeling more than a little angry, Hattie yanked the door open.

But she saw no one.

And all she heard was the chirping of the cicadas.

She was just about to go back to bed when she glanced down and noticed the raggedy burlap sack on her front porch. She picked it up and looked around before bringing it into the parlor.

The sack was heavy and something inside of it rattled when she moved it. Curious, she untied the cord at the top and peeked inside.

Then she screamed at the top of her lungs and fainted.

Clem came downstairs just as Hattie hit the floor. He ran over and helped her onto the sofa.

"What's wrong?" he asked as he rubbed her hand.

Hattie, unable to speak, pointed to the sack.

Clem walked over and looked inside.

"Mother of God!" he exclaimed as he retied the cord.

Hattie watched as he hurried back upstairs. Five minutes later, he was dressed and heading out the door with the sack in his hands.

"I'm goin' over to see the sheriff," he called over his shoulder. "Don't wait up!"

Big Jim Gerber was a burly man with a level disposition. He'd been the sheriff for 18 years and thought he'd seen everything. Nothing seemed to rattle or surprise him. Nothing, that is, until Clem entered the station with the sack.

Jim nodded.

He'd seen such a sack before and had a sickening feeling about what it contained..

"This was left on my porch, Jim," Clem said as he placed the sack on the desk.

Jim and his deputy, Harper, opened the sack and dumped the contents onto the desk. Both of them winced. Jim stared at the contents in disbelief, then looked at Clem.

"You can go home now, Clem. I'll see that this gets to the right folks," he said.

Clem nodded and hurried from the station. Jim plopped back down in his chair while Harper shook his head.

"That's the second one, Jim," Harper said.

"I can count, Harper," Jim snapped. "This has gotten beyond anything we can handle ourselves. We need help and fast."

"What are you gonna do?" asked Harper.

"I'm going to write a letter to that Hunter feller in New Orleans and ask him to come up here," Jim replied.

"Think he can help?" asked Harper.

"If he can't, then *nobody* can—not even God," Jim said. "Put that back in the sack and place it in the safe with the other one. We'll tell their families after we figure out what's going on around here."

Five days later, Hunter and Lorena returned home from lunch to find an all-too-familiar blue business card tacked to their front door. The card was from Minerva DuPres, the reigning voodoo queen of New Orleans. Written on the back of it were the words:

YOU'RE NEEDED.

Hunter showed it to Lorena.

"Let's round up Jean-Paul and head over to the temple," he said.

An hour later, Hunter, Lorena and a slightly hung-over DuCassal walked into Minerva's temple on Chartres. As usual, there were four cups, four saucers, a pot of herbal tea and a platter of fresh spice cookies waiting for them on the parlor table.

Minerva was already seated in her favorite chair, a high-backed Victorian style wicker with flowery cushions. She smiled as they sat down.

"It's about time you got here," she said.

"What's up?" asked Hunter as he helped himself to a cookie.

"I got a letter from Big Jim Gerber. He's the sheriff up in Baton Rouge. He asked me to send you up to help him," Minerva said.

"With what? Vampires? Rougarous? Ghosts?" asked Hunter.

"He doesn't know. Big Jim is a very level headed and resourceful man. He never asks anyone for help—not that much ever happens up in Baton Rouge," Minerva said. "So I was very surprised to receive his letter."

"I know Big Jim. If he's come up against something he can't handle, it must be real bad," DuCassal said as he nibbled on a cookie. "Real bad."

"So what's the problem?" asked Hunter.

"Someone or something has been stealing little girls away from their families, killing them, then returning their bones in sacks," Minerva said as she handed him the letter.

Hunter perused it and whistled.

"We'll ride up there as soon as possible," he said.

"We can leave two days from now," Lorena added. "After I complete some personal business."

Minerva smiled.

"Hannah Morii?" she asked.

Lorena's jaw dropped.

Minerva laughed.

"No, child. I didn't read your mind. Hannah came in here a month ago and asked my advice on whether she should go through with it. I told her that only she could decide such a thing for herself, but I also offered to pray for her to assure it goes well," she said. "Is it?"

"So far, so good," Lorena replied.

"But you still feel uneasy about it. I can see that in your eyes," Minerva observed. "If it is of any consolation, bear in mind that what you are doing will one day save Hannah's life. And remember—it was *she* who asked you to do this and her motives were purely unselfish."

Lorena smiled and nodded.

She didn't bring up the fact that their session that morning had lasted over an hour because both she and Hannah had given in to their primal urges and taken their relationship to another level. Lorena also knew that the next two times, those urges would be stronger.

"What do you think is terrorizing Baton Rouge?" asked Hunter.

"I don't have a clue. Whatever it is, it likes to eat little girls," Minerva replied.

"So do I—well, not *little* girls exactly," DuCassal remarked.

Minerva shook her head and looked at Hunter.

"Was he *always* like this?" she asked.

Hunter shrugged.

"I don't really remember," he said.

"Lucky you," Minerva said.

Before they left, Lorena made her seventh and final visit to Hannah Morii. She found upstairs on her bed with a big smile on her lips. This time, she was completely nude.

When they were finished more than an hour later, Lorena got up and dressed. Hannah lay on the bed smiling up at her.

"In a few minutes, you'll lapse into a deep, easy sleep," she said. "It should last about three days."

"And when I wake?" Hannah asked.

Lorena smiled down at her.

"If the transformation goes well, you'll begin to notice several changes. Each day, you'll feel more and more different. Some changes will be very subtle. Others will be quite dramatic. Within three weeks, you will a full blooded vampire," she whispered.

She donned her cloak and left the shop, making sure to lock the front door behind her when she did. Hannah's almost comatose slumber would give her body time to adapt to the changes in her cellular structure and metabolism.

Lorena had never turned anyone before. It felt strange to take the blood of a friend, but Hannah offered herself of her own free will.

She saw Hunter and DuCassal standing outside.

"Is it done?" Hunter asked as they walked down the street.

"Yes. Everything went well. When we return from Baton Rouge, Hannah will be fully transformed," Lorena said.

Hunter noticed a tone of resignation in her voice.

"What's wrong?" he asked.

She clutched his arm and smiled.

"Nothing. I just did something that I swore I would never do. I created another vampire," she replied. "And I drank the blood of a friend. That's something else I vowed never to do."

"It was Hannah's idea. And you did it for a good cause," Hunter said assuringly.

Then he suddenly stiffened and blinked his eyes several times. Lorena looked at him and realized that another vision or memory had just flashed through his mind.

"What did you see?" she asked.

"I saw myself signing a contract and handing it to the Devil. Then I heard him say it was the first time anyone had ever made a deal with him for a *good* cause," Hunter replied. "It lasted only a second or two. Then it was gone."

DuCassal raided an eyebrow.

"*You* made a contract with the Devil?" he queried in disbelief.

"I'm not sure. It's like part of a strange dream," Hunter said. "I don't even know if that was me in the vision."

"It *must* be you, mon ami. You certainly wouldn't have someone else's memories enter your mind, would you?" DuCassal asked.

Hunter shook his head.

"But what does it all mean, Jean-Paul?" he asked.

"What does it matter? If it actually happened, it must have taken place centuries ago. If it's of any importance to you now, I'm sure you'll remember when the time comes," DuCassal assured him. "Right now, we have work to do."

They followed Esplanade past City Park and Bayou St. John. When the street ended, they took the road that went around Lake Ponchartrain. This took the better part of the morning and afternoon, so they stopped to eat at a small oyster bar. Afterward, they continued to follow the road until they reached the small, picturesque fishing village of Poitiers which hugged the edge of the lake.

Poitiers was one of the newer villages, having been founded 150 years earlier by several fishermen. It soon evolved into a nice weekend retreat for city dwellers trying to escape the summer heat.

The buildings were mostly well-kept one story wooden cottages, several of which also had their own docks. There were also three small inns and a smattering of shops and restaurants. The narrow streets were cobblestone and lined with live oaks whose branches intertwined to form protective canopies from the sun.

They spent the night at the Dew Drop Inn, which was owned and operated by a good friend of DuCassal's named Becky DuChamps and her young sons Billy and Todd.

Todd was just 12 years old and he spent at least an hour quizzing them about what it was like to be a Slayer. He was especially fascinated with Lorena. She was the first vampire he'd ever met and he was absolutely taken by her beauty.

Wednesday morning in New Orleans.

Mary Figgins, the head teller of the Bayou Bank, looked up and smiled at the tall, rather distinguished looking gentleman standing at the counter. She had just finished counting out the large bag of gold coins he'd handed her to open a new account. There were 500 in all, and each of them weighed at least an ounce. The man didn't look particularly muscular and she wondered how on Earth he had managed to carry the sack with such apparent ease.

"That converts to 500,000 Louisiana dollars," she said as she filled out his deposit slip and passed it to him. "Just sign on the bottom line and we'll activate your account, Mr. Considine."

The man reached for the slip. As he did, he briefly made contact with her fingertips. She watched as he signed it, passed it back and thanked her for her trouble. Then he turned and walked out of the bank.

The moment he left, she began to feel slightly dizzy. A few moments later, she began to perspire profusely and her knees wobbled. She barely made it to her desk before she passed out.

When she came to an hour later, she was surrounded by several of her concerned co-workers. Mary smiled weakly at them.

"I don't know what's come over me," she said. "I must be coming down with something."

As Mr. Considine walked through along Canal Street, he "accidentally" collided with an unsuspecting young woman with dark hair. The collision almost knocked her off her feet and would have if he hadn't grabbed her with both hands. They both smiled and apologized to each other. Then Mr. Considine melted into the crowd. As soon as he was out of sight, the woman he had collided with became so dizzy, she was forced to find a bench to rest on.

"I must be coming down with the flu," she thought as she watched the street spin around her.

Hannah Morii slowly opened her eyes and winced at the bright sunlight beaming through her window. She rolled to an upright position and looked around. She felt a little bit drained but otherwise alright. She got up and went to the bathroom. As she splashed water on her face she looked into the mirror, she stared at her reflection.

"I still look the same," she said.

She then checked the side of her neck. She was surprised to see that the bite marks were completely gone.

"So soon?" she thought as she brushed her teeth.

When she was through, she rinsed her mouth then looked at them closely in the mirror to see if she had somehow grown fangs.

She hadn't.

"Well, Lorena did say the fangs would appear only when I intended to use them," she said as she brushed her long hair. "And when I needed to feed."

How long before *that* happens?

Would she be able to handle it?

She took a deep breath and slowly exhaled.

"I guess I'll just have to get used to it," she said. "Now that I've done this, I can't undo it."

She was still naked.

She walked back into the bathroom and turned on her shower. She was sticky from the humidity and still oh-so-tired.

Drained was a better word for it, she told herself. She knew that she should still be asleep. Lorena told her she'd sleep for at least three straight days. Yet here she was awake and showering.

But it didn't last.

Almost as soon as she dried herself off, she began to feel weak and dizzy. She sat down on the bed and decided to take another short nap.

She wouldn't wake for another 48 hours.

Hunter, Lorena and DuCassal arrived in Baton Rouge late Thursday afternoon. DuCassal, being familiar with the city, led them right to the police station where a large, burly man and several uniformed deputies were seated on the front porch.

DuCassal waved as they rode up.

"Big Jim! We are here!" he shouted.

Big Jim smiled and ran over as they dismounted.

"I can't tell you how happy I am to see you folks," Big Jim said as he shook their hands. "I am sorta surprised to see *you* Jean-Paul. Since when are you a Slayer?"

"Since Charles returned to New Orleans. We just picked up where had left off a long, long time ago," DuCassal said. "So what is this about someone stealing little girls?"

"It's a real tragedy," Big Jim said as they entered the station. "There's somebody out there who likes to kidnap small girls then return their bones and other articles in sacks. I've never seen anything like this in all my years of sheriffing."

"You say they return the bones?" Hunter asked.

Big Jim nodded.

"Yep—and there ain't a sign of any meat on them at all. Hell, they all look like they've been boiled or something," he said.

He looked at his deputy.

"Harper—go down to the safe and fetch those sacks," he said.

Harper nodded and left the room. A minute later, he returned with two sacks, which he placed on Big Jim's desk.

Hunter reached out and opened one of the sacks. Then he carefully removed the contents and placed them on the top of the desk. The remains consisted of the stripped, boiled bones of a small girl, skull fragments, locks of red hair and neatly folded clothes and a pair of tiny shoes. Hunter picked up several bones, one at a time, and examined each closely.

"The meat appears to have been scraped from each bone. This one here has teeth marks. There's no sign of tendons, sinew or even cartilage," he said. "From the size of the bones, I'd say she was no more than five years old."

"Four actually," Jim said.

"Who was she?" Hunter asked.

"Lizzie Borden," Jim replied.

Hunter gave him a raised eyebrow.

Jim smiled.

"No, really. She was snatched from the front yard of her parents' house on the night of May 24th. Her parents positively identified the clothes and shoes. The remains were left on the front porch of Augusta Diamond two weeks ago."

"Is she related to the child in any way?" asked Lorena.

"Nope. Didn't even know her," Jim said.

"Why dump the bones there?" DuCassal asked. "It doesn't make any sense."

"I'll say!" Jim agreed.

Harper opened the second sack and handed it to Hunter. He poured the remains onto the table and shook his head. This skeleton was even smaller and the bones had the same markings.

"That was Linda Jones, age two," Jim explained. "She was taken from her bedroom on the night of May 25th. That sack was placed on the Taliafiero porch one week ago. They have no connection at all to the Jones family."

"That makes even less sense," Hunter said.

"I told you this case was off the wall," Jim reminded him. "I gets worse."

"Go on," Hunter urged.

"Two other kids, also girls, were taken during the same week. One was Clementine Martin, age 3. The other was Willie Taylor, age 4. Both were snatched from their homes in the middle of the night without their parents hearing or seeing a thing."

"That's four. Were any others kidnapped either before or since?" asked Hunter.

"Nope," Jim said.

"Do you have a calendar?" asked Lorena.

Big Jim pointed to the one on the wall behind her. Lorena walked over and checked the dates.

"The kidnappings took place during the height of the full moon," she said.

Hunter picked up several bones and cracked them in two. He showed them to Jim.

"No marrow," the sheriff observed.

"Someone—or something—sucked it out after the bones were boiled," Hunter said.

"You mean they've been cooked and eaten?" asked Jim.

"That's a safe bet," Hunter replied.

"That rules out vampires or werewolves. Vampires only go for the blood and werewolves never stop to cook their victims," Lorena said.

"Demons?" asked DuCassal.

"Maybe—but unlikely," Hunter said as he paced.

"We're dealing with someone who kidnaps little girls during a full moon then later cooks and eats them," he said. "From the way the bones were prepared and the clothes were neatly folded, it appears that the children were used in some sort of ritual."

"Voodoo?" asked Jim.

"More like witchcraft or black magic. Voodoo ceremonies don't require human sacrifices," Hunter said. "The full moon must have something to do with a specific time. That's why the kidnappings stopped when the moon left its full phase."

He looked at the piles of bones and sighed.

"And when the ritual is over, the kidnapper eats them," he said sadly.

"At least they aren't being *wasted*," DuCassal remarked.

This earned him a hard stomp to his foot from Lorena. He jumped back and hopped around a few times to show he was hurt. She just smirked at him. Big Jim shook his head.

"You haven't changed a bit, Jean-Paul," he said.

"Why kids?" asked Harper.

"Maybe they are more tender and easier to cook than adults," DuCassal offered as he moved out of Lorena's range. "And little girls must be more tender than little boys."

"That's just sick!" Jim declared.

Hunter nodded.

"Very," he agreed. "The kidnappings occurred two weeks ago. So far, two sacks of bones have turned up, one in each successive week."

"One week apart to the date of their kidnappings," Jim pointed out.

"He must be able to stretch a child over several meals," DuCassal said. "I wonder what side dishes one would prepare to go with a child?"

Lorena shot him a disgusted look.

Hunter, Jim and Harper all groaned.

DuCassal simply shrugged.

"That *is* disturbing!" Lorena declared.

"You mean me or the kidnappers?" DuCassal asked.

"Both!" she said.

"I just thought of something even more disturbing," Hunter said. "Is the kidnapper eating the kids himself or are they being fed to something?"

"Wow! That is a terrifying thought!" Jim said as it hit home.

"Amen to that!" added Harper.

Hunter stepped to the window and stared out at the vast swamp in the distance.

"Four were taken. Two have been returned. That means there are still two little girls out there who are in desperate need of a rescue," he said.

"That's an awfully big swamp out there. How are you going to find them?" asked Jim.

Hunter turned to him and smiled.

"I won't find them---but Lorena will," he declared.

"Where did the most recent kidnapping occur?" she asked.

"At the Borden house," Big Jim said.

"Take us there," said Hunter.

The Bordens lived in a small, white clapboard house with a green shingle roof. It was surrounded by a low wooden, picket fence and several flower gardens. Big Jim walked up and knocked on the front door.

Jack Borden, Lizzie's father, let them in as Big Jim made the introductions. They were joined in the parlor by Jack's wife, Elsie.

"This young lady here is going to help us find whoever took Lizzie," Big Jim said.

"Where was Lizzie when you last saw her?" asked Lorena.

"She was asleep in her bedroom," Elsie replied. "I'll take you to it."

Elsie led her to a pretty, neatly furnished room with a small, canopied bed. Lorena looked around and nodded.

"Please leave me," she said.

Elsie left and shut the door behind her. Lorena sat down on Lizzie's bed and closed her eyes. Ten minutes later, she returned to the parlor where everyone was waiting.

"Did you see anything?" asked Hunter.

Lorena nodded.

"What was it?" asked Big Jim.

"She was lured away by someone she wanted to play with. I saw another child with her and they seemed to be holding hands and skipping toward the swamp," Lorena said. "That's why no one heard screams. She didn't feel that she was in any danger. She was just going off to play with her new friend."

"You mean the kidnapper's a kid?" asked Jim.

"Or someone who *looked* like a child," Hunter said. "We may be dealing with someone who can change his or her appearance at will."

"That sounds more like a witch or demon, mon ami," DuCassal said.

"Can you locate the lair?" asked Hunter.

"I think so," Lorena answered.

"It's too late now. We'll start tomorrow," Hunter said as he watched the setting sun.

"Good idea. Only a complete fool would go into those swamps at night," Jim agreed. "It's crawling with gators and poisonous snakes. Some folks even say that a fifolet lives out there."

"Is there a hotel nearby?" Hunter asked.

"Right up the street from the station," Jim replied.

"Thanks. We'll see you first thing in the morning," Hunter said as they mounted up.

Lorena noticed that Harper was looking at her kind of strangely. She smiled.

"Yes, vampires can and do move about freely during daylight," she assured him. "As long as I wear dark glasses and keep much of my body protected from direct sunlight, I am fine. But I am at my best after sunset."

Harper smiled.

"Thanks, Miss. I was just curious," he said.

She laughed.

"I understand. Most people are surprised to see me in full daylight. But you would be shocked to learn how many of us walk among you at all hours of the day and night," she said.

"So real vampires are nothing like the ones in those old stories?" asked Jim.

"Not at all," Lorena replied. "We don't sleep in coffins. We can't change into bats or wolves or smoke. And we certainly don't run from crosses or avoid going into churches and other holy places. Most of all, we are *not* walking corpses. We are very much alive."

Jim laughed.

"You certainly don't look like a corpse!" he said. "In fact, you look way more alive than most of the people *in* this town."

"And you're a damned sight prettier than any of the women around here," Harper added.

Lorena blushed.

"Merci," she said with a smile.

Jim looked at Hunter.

"What about you, Hunter? Are you like Jean-Paul here? This guy hasn't changed a bit since my great grand daddy knew him," he said.

"Charles and I go back many centuries. We are *very old* friends," DuCassal said.

"What's it like to live forever?" asked Jim.

"I don't know. I have not yet lived forever," DuCassal said. "Life, no matter how short or long, is what one makes of it. It's how well one lives that matters. And as you can see, I have lived very well."

Jim nodded.

"Just how old are you, Jean-Paul?" he asked.

"I don't know. I stopped counting the candles on my birthday cake centuries ago. Does it matter?" DuCassal replied.

"I suppose not," Jim said. "Uh, can you die?"

"Everyone dies sooner or later," DuCassal said.

"Even us?" asked Hunter.

DuCassal shrugged.

"That remains to be seen. But I am in no great hurry to find out," he said as he mounted his horse.

They rode over to the hotel and checked in for the week. After a hearty meal in the hotel dining room, they bathed and retired for the night.

At three a.m., everyone in the hotel was rudely awakened by the loud sound of shattering glass. Hunter, Lorena and DuCassal leaped out of bed and hurried downstairs. When they arrived, Maggie, the night clerk and three other workers were standing in the lobby staring down at a large burlap sack lying amid shards of broken glass.

"Somebody threw this right through our front door," Maggie said.

Hunter knelt and opened the sack. He shook his head and gently dumped the pitiful contents onto the floor. It was the remains of another missing child along with a badly scrawled note.

Hunter picked up the note and showed it to the others while Maggie sent the bellman over to tell Big Jim.

"I know yer heer but ye'll never find me," the note read.

"Want to bet?" Hunter said as he crumpled the note and tossed it into a nearby waste basket.

He turned to Lorena and DuCassal.

"Get ready. It'll be dawn soon," he said.

New Orleans.

Inspector Valmonde stepped onto his front porch and picked up the paper the delivery man had tossed onto it. He broke the string and unrolled it.

A banner headline proclaimed that New Orleans was in the grip of an influenza epidemic. The story said that over 50 cases had been reported within the last six days. What made this unusual was the fact that it wasn't flu season.

And all of the reported cases came on quite suddenly and without warning. The paper said that according to the Health Department, this strain, although it hit its victims hard at first, was actually very mild. In fact, most of the symptoms were gone within 48 hours or so.

Valmonde shrugged and rolled the paper back up.

It was Sunday.

His first day off in six years.

He didn't give a damn about any old flu epidemic anyway.

Big Jim and Harper hurried over to the hotel. Hunter, Lorena and DuCassal were dressed and waiting in the lobby. The sack containing the bones was on the check-in counter.

"Is that the sack?" Jim asked.

"That's it," Hunter said as he handed it to him.

Jim examined the remains.

"This is probably the Martin girl," he said. "What's your next move?"

"Lorena will try to track the missing girls as soon as the sun is up," Hunter replied.

"That won't be for another hour," Jim said.

"Is there a place we can get a good breakfast?" DuCassal asked.

"Mary Ann's Diner is just two blocks down the street from here. It's a real good, too," Harper suggested.

"In that case, we'll see you after breakfast, Jim," Hunter said.

An hour later, they met Big Jim and Harper at the station. Big Jim looked at Lorena.

"Where do you want to start, Miss?" he asked.

"The Borden house is closest. We'll start there," she replied.

They walked over to the house and into the back yard. Lorena walked to the child's bedroom window, stopped and concentrated. Then she began to walk.

"Let's go!" Hunter said.

They walked to the city limits, then turned south and into the swamp. At the edge of the swamp, Lorena paused to get her bearings. After a second or two, she pointed.

"They went that way," she stated and headed deeper into the swamp.

"Are you sure?" Big Jim asked.

"Lorena is *never* wrong, sheriff," Hunter assured him.

About a mile into the swamp, they came to a small clearing. Lorena stopped and looked around as if she was lost.

"What's wrong?" asked Hunter.

"The trail ends here," she replied.

Hunter looked around at the open patch of greenish-yellow grass.

"Are you sure?" he asked.

"Positive. It ends in the middle of this clearing," she replied.

"But there's nothing out here," Harper said.

"Nothing at all," added DuCassal.

"I must have missed something. Let's got to the second child's home and try again. Maybe it will lead somewhere else," Lorena said almost in frustration.

It wasn't like her to lose a trail. She had an inborn sense that always led her directly to whomever she was hunting. She looked at Hunter and shrugged.

They walked back to town and over to the Taylor house.

Again she concentrated.

Again she picked up on the image of an older child leading the toddler off into the swamp. She looked around and nodded.

"I've picked up the trail," she said as she headed off toward the swamp.

Twenty minutes later, they found themselves standing in the exact same clearing. Lorena shook her head, then let out a frustrated groan.

Hunter removed his hat and scratched his head as he looked around. There was nothing at all in the clearing. No path led into or out of it. There were no foot prints save their own. He looked at Lorena.

"This is where it ends," she assured him.

"Since both trails led us here, we must be in the right place. But there's nothing out here," Hunter said.

"This is nuts!" Big Jim said. "Those kids just didn't vanish into thin air."

"They didn't," Hunter said.

Lorena saw the smirk on his face and realized he was onto something.

"Each child was taken around the same time, right?" Hunter asked.

"Yeah. They went missing around three in the morning," Big Jim agreed. "So?"

"All four were led to this spot. Then they vanished. And all three of sets of remains turned up around the same time, one week apart," Hunter said. "If this is where they were taken, then something must happen here around three a.m."

"I see where you're going with this, Charles," DuCassal smiled. "Whatever it is must only last for an hour or so. Then it vanishes, too."

"Along with those kids," Jim said.

"The logical thing to do is stand vigil out here around that time each morning to see if anything shows up. Once we see what it is, we'll be able to deal with it," Hunter said. "We may have another House of the Rising Sun on our hands."

"Another phantom house—or worse," DuCassal added.

Big Jim nodded.

"Those sacks turned up on the same night each week. The last one turned up yesterday. That mean it should be six more days before something else happens," he said.

"When it does, we'll be waiting," Hunter said. "We'll begin the vigil tonight. If the last child is still alive, we have to get in there and save her before she ends up in a sack."

"What are the chances that she's still alive?" asked Harper.

Hunter shook his head.

"That all depends on the circumstances," he said.

"And if she's dead?" asked Big Jim.

"Then may God help whatever's behind this," Hunter replied.

CHAPTER TWO:
House of Gingerbread?

New Orleans.

Valmonde sat at his desk in the Basin Street station eating beignet and drinking coffee while he perused the morning paper. The good news was the strange flu epidemic seemed to have tapered off as no new cases had been reported for the last two days. The bad news was it was raining.

Hard.

A nasty storm had blown in from the gulf and inundated New Orleans. There was so much water that the ancient sewer system had trouble containing it all and several areas of the city were now flooded.

But not too badly.

"Oh, well. At least the storms keep the crime rate down," Valmonde said as he turned the page.

That's when he saw the story about a mystery man who deposited $500,000 in gold coins in the Bayou Bank and disappeared.

"That's typical," Valmonde thought. "Lots of folks drop their fortunes off in New Orleans then vanish for a few years. I'm sure that guy's no different. Someone always comes back to claim it."

The "mystery man" hadn't exactly vanished.

At that very moment, he was also looking through the newspaper. This time, he was reading the section that contained articles of patients who were in the terminal wing of New Orleans Hospital.

When he came to a certain paragraph, he circled it with a pencil. Then he tore off that part of the page, folded it and stuck it into his vest pocket.

"He will do nicely," the man thought as he tossed the paper into a dumpster and walked over to Rampart Street.

Hannah Morii finally woke up from her deep slumber. It was past sunset and she felt like she had been supercharged. She sat up and leaped to her feet. And she did it surprisingly fast.

She smiled.

It was almost time to begin her patrol through the darker corners of the city. She heard the rain beating against her bedroom window and pushed aside the curtain to peer out at the street. Water was rushing along Royal like a raging river.

And the street was empty.

"It's the perfect night to see what's changed inside of me," she thought.

She slipped into her black outfit and armed herself with her katana as usual. She walked downstairs, took her cloak down from the peg on the wall behind the counter and draped it over herself.

That's when she realized that she hadn't turned on the light.

She also realized that she didn't need to as she could see clearly, even though the shop was mostly pitch black.

Hannah smiled.

"Lorena said I'd have heightened senses. I think I'll test them," she aid as she left the shop.

Three a.m.

A lone owl hooted in the distance to break the eerie quiet of swamp the as they entered the clearing. A pale, crescent moon provided the only light as they sat down in the grass and waited for something to happen.

DuCassal nonchalantly munched on a gator tail po'boy he'd brought with him. Hunter and Lorena sat back-to-back and watched the clearing.

Minutes became an hour.

By now, hundreds of cicadas had filled the air with their mating calls as the early morning symphony began.

DuCassal yawned.

He glanced at the center of the clearing and jumped to his feet as the faint outline of a house began to materialize.

Hunter and Lorena were also on their feet. They watched in silence as a run-down, wood and earth two story shack began to solidify. It had a high pitched roof made of rotted shingles, half of which appeared to have sunken inward; a bent chimney, and several dirty, half-shuttered windows. The front door leaned creakily from a single hinge and there was a smaller wooden shack with smoke coming from its chimney to the rear.

"You were right, mon ami," DuCassal said. "This is why all of the trails led directly to this clearing."

"Let's check it out," Hunter said as he drew his revolver.

DuCassal slid two shells into his shotgun, locked it, and nodded.

"I'll search the smaller shack," he said as he walked off.

Hunter and Lorena were about to approach the house when it suddenly underwent a second transformation.

Instead of the run-down hovel, what stood before them now was something straight out of a fairy tale. The house was now a lovely Victorian era cottage with ornate wooden trim, a thatched roof and flower boxes in all of the windows. The front door had become a quaint, well-maintained arched door with a silver bell on a cord next to it.

Hunter and Lorena stared at each other, then slowly walked toward the house.

"It looks like a gingerbread house from a child's story book," Lorena remarked. "It's beautiful!"

"It would *have* to be to lure little girls inside," Hunter said. "The cottage is just an illusion that conceals the real house."

Lorena reached out and touched the wall.

"It feels real enough," she said.

"It's a *good* illusion," Hunter said with a smirk.

Just then, DuCassal raced over to them.

"I think you had better have a look inside that shack," he suggested.

They followed him to the shack. As soon as they drew close, the smell of roasting meat caught their attention. Hunter looked at DuCassal.

"What's in there?" he asked.

"I think you had better see for yourself, Charles," DuCassal said. "But steel yourself. It isn't pretty."

Hunter eased the door open and winced.

"Mother of God!" he exclaimed as he looked around.

There was a low, smoky fire burning in a pit, over which was suspended an iron cage. Inside the cage were several strange-looking cuts of meat dangling from hooks. They were obviously curing over the fire.

Several other cuts of meat, already cured, hung from the rafters. There were also several large Mason jars on a nearby shelf. Hunter picked one up and shook it. When a human eyeball looked back at him from the murky liquid, he threw it against the wall in disgust. When the jar shattered, it sent four more eyeballs rolling across the floor.

"This is a *smokehouse!*" he said.

The loathing in tone was obvious to Lorena and DuCassal.

Lorena looked at the meat in the cage and shook her head sadly.

"These are human remains," she said. "But where are the bones?"

"Over here in this cauldron," DuCassal said as he pointed to the large, metal pot sitting on an open fire. "It appears as if they have been boiling for hours."

"When we find this monster, we kill it," Hunter said sternly.

"It will be a pleasure, mon ami," DuCassal agreed.

"And I'd love to boil him in this very cauldron!" Lorena almost growled.

They walked back to the cottage. Hunter tried the back door. To his surprise, it was unlocked. He cautiously eased the door inward and stepped inside with his revolver at the ready. After his eyes grew accustomed to the dim light, he waved for the others to come in.

The inside of the cottage was nothing like the outside. They found themselves standing in a dirty, run-down excuse for a kitchen with a rickety old wood plank table, two wobbly wooden chairs, and badly hung cupboards. A large, greasy-looking cast iron stove stood against one wall and there was an old oil lantern on the table.

DuCassal lit the lantern and walked through the front parlor, which was just as run-down as the kitchen. He set the lantern on the window sill and smiled.

"That's so the owner of this 'mansion' can find his way home," he joked.

"And to announce our presence," Hunter said. "Let's check out the second floor."

The stairway was in poor condition with a loose handrail and uneven steps that creaked loudly beneath their feet. The upstairs landing led to three wooden doors. Hunter looked around and pointed at two of the doors. DuCassal went for the one on the left. Lorena took the one on the right.

Hunter waited.

They returned quickly and shook their heads. He nodded and walked to the next door. He put his ear against and heard something squeaking like springs in an old mattress. He stepped back and kicked the door open.

Directly in front of them was a large bed with brass rails. On top of the bed was a small, shivering girl. The girl was completely naked. Her wrists and ankles were secured to the bedposts by ropes and she had a gag over her mouth.

Hunter took a step forward and hesitated.

"Something doesn't feel right," he said.

Lorena ignored him and raced for the child. She removed the gag and untied each rope. The girl immediately hugged her tight and began to sob. Lorena held her close and stroked her hair.

"There, there, little one! You're safe now. We've come to save you," she said softly.

That's when the child glared menacingly at Hunter and made the most evil-looking smile he'd ever seen. Before he could react, the little girl transformed herself into a hideous, gray-skinned, scaly-skinned creature with dull red eyes, jagged yellow teeth and a grotesque hump on its back. It immediately seized Lorena's hair and attempted to sink its teeth into her neck. Lorena rammed her thumbs into its eyes and tossed the now howling thing to the floor.

It sprang up and charged right at Hunter only to be sent crashing to the floor again by a powerful left cross. It hissed, snarled and sprang at him again. This time, he emptied his revolver into its chest. The thing struck the floor amid a shower of its own blood and screamed and growled in pain and anger. Before it could get back up, DuCassal placed both barrels of his shotgun against its face and pulled the triggers. The shot splattered bits of flesh, bone and gray matter throughout the room.

To everyone's amazement, it was still trying to get back up and its shattered face was slowly reforming. Lorena grabbed the ropes from the bed and quickly bound the creature's hands and feet. Then she gave it a good hard kick in the head that appeared to quiet it down.

Unable to continue the battle, the creature slowly reverted to its true form: a grizzled, scraggly-haired old crone with several large sores on her body that oozed pus.

"Just as I thought—a witch!" Hunter said as he looked down at her.

"And a damned ugly one at that!" DuCassal added.

"You're not exactly an Adonis yourself, asshole," the witch snarled in her gravelly voice. "When I get free of these ropes, I'll make you all pay dearly for this."

"I'm a little short on cash. Will you accept an I.O.U.?" DuCassal joked.

Hunter put his foot on her throat and glared at her.

"You're hardly in a position to threaten us or anyone else. And I'm going to make sure that you never harm another child ever again," he said menacingly.

"She appears to be bullet proof, mon ami. How are we going to get rid of her?" asked DuCassal.

"The same way they got rid of witches during the Dark Ages," Hunter said as he dragged her to her feet by her stringy hair.

The witch yowled in agony as he dragged her down the steps and out through the back door to the smokehouse. He kicked the door open, hauled her inside and impaled her on one of the meat hooks. Lorena entered next and used a length of chain from the suspended cage to secure the witch to the post while she cursed and struggled to get free. Hunter kicked her in the chest to knock the wind out of her.

He took a bottle of blessed oil from his pocket and poured it over the witch. Then he struck a match.

"Any last words?" he asked.

"Fuck you!" the witch swore.

"Not on your best day," he replied as he ignited the oil.

She writhed in agony and emitted a series of loud howls and screams that reverberated through the swamp. Hunter, Lorena and DuCassal stepped out side and watched as the flames consumed both the smokehouse and the witch. Within an hour, all that remained was a pile of smoldering ashes.

They heard a loud creak behind them and turned to see the cottage revert to the run-down hovel then slowly fall to pieces.

"It's over, mes amis," DuCassal declared. "Ding, dong, the witch is dead!"

"And we didn't have to drop a house on her," Hunter said with a smile.

Lorena cast them a puzzled look. DuCassal laughed.

"It's from an old movie of the First Age," he said. "I'm surprised that you remember it, Charles."

"Me, too," Hunter said. "Let's go home."

Two a.m.

John Rush staggered out of Pat O'Brien's and slowly wove his way along North Peters until he reached Decatur. On the corner of Wilkinson, he happened to get jostled by a tall, self-important looking man in a dark suit.

The amount of alcohol he'd consumed (and consumed him) caused him to take a misguided swing at the stranger with his fist.

An hour later, six young women also left the bar. When the reached Decatur and Wilkinson, they spotted a man lying face-down in the street. Thinking he may be hurt, they rushed over to see if they could help. One of the women turned the man over.

Then all of them emitted a series of high-pitched, terrified screams that emptied out a nearby saloon and quickly brought several officers to the scene.

Twenty minutes later, Valmonde and two of his men arrived to see what the trouble was. One of the officers who was already there, pointed to the corpse. Valmonde looked at the withered, almost leathery face and bulging eyes and cringed.

The man looked as if he'd been dried out in a desert for a thousand years. Valmonde squatted down ad touched the man's face.

"There ain't a drop of moisture in this old boy," he said. "It's like he had the life sucked completely out of him."

"You think a vampire got him?" asked Sam.

"No tellin' what got him. Tell the ambulance boys to take him to the morgue," Valmonde said as he stood up and looked around.

"Hunter sure picked a bad time to leave town," he said as he walked back to his carriage.

Hunter, Lorena and DuCassal returned to New Orleans three days later.

Weary and dusty from their long ride, they nonetheless decided to check in with Valmonde before heading home. The Inspector smiled when they entered his office.

"Am I glad to see you folks!" he said as he walked over to greet them.

"That's usually a bad sign," Hunter said as they shook hands. "What's happened?"

"Somethin' really weird. Let's head over to the hospital. There's somethin' in the morgue I want to show you," Valmonde said.

Fifteen minutes later, they were looking down into the cold, dead eyes a very emaciated corpse on a slab.

"What's the cause of death?" Hunter asked.

"According to the doctor, the cause of death is total dehydration. The coroner said she couldn't find a single drop of fluid anywhere in this man's body. She said it looked like he'd been mummified," Valmonde said.

Hunter nodded.

"Is he the only victim?" he asked.

"So far. Why? You expectin' more?" Valmonde asked.

"There's a distinct possibility of that," Hunter said.

"So, I take you've seen somethin' like this before?" Valmonde asked.

"Several times. But only in parts of Europe," Hunter said as he paced. "Who was he?"

"Accordin' to his wallet, his name's John Rush. He's from California," Valmonde answered. "He just arrived in New Orleans a few nights ago."

"Well, this is as good a place as any to die," DuCassal said.

"He didn't just die, Jean-Paul. He was *murdered*," Hunter said.

"Are you thinking what I am thinking, mon cher?" asked Lorena.

"I am—and I hope like Hell I'm wrong," Hunter said.

DuCassal looked at them.

"The Baron you mentioned?" he asked.

They both nodded.

"This is normally what's left of one of his victims—when he decides to kill for some reason," Hunter replied.

"Who's this Baron fella?" asked Valmonde. "He some kind of vampire?"

"The worst kind," Hunter said. "If he's in New Orleans, he could be anywhere. He's impossible to find unless he wants to be found. He either leaves his victims feeling sick and weak for a few days or like this."

"Weak and sick? You mean like they have the flu or somethin'?" Valmonde asked.

"That's right. Why?" Hunter replied.

"While you were away, we had a minor flu epidemic. At least that's what the boys at the Health Department called it," Valmonde answered.

"How many people were affected?" asked Lorena.

"Around 100 or so. The epidemic lasted about a week," Valmonde replied.

"That sounds like something the Baron would do," Hunter said.

"I take you've run into him before?" Valmonde asked.

"Several times," Hunter said.

"And he's still alive?" asked the Inspector.

Hunter and Lorena nodded.

"Danm! If *you* couldn't kill him, this Baron must be Hell on wheels," Valmonde remarked.

"He's worse than that, Chief," Lorena said. "He's also the monster who turned *me*. I'm not sure if I should thank him or kill him for that, either. Mostly, I'd like to kill him."

"*If* he can be killed," DuCassal said.

"Everything can be killed. You just have to find the right combination of things to kill him with," Hunter said. "If he is here in New Orleans, he's made one Hell of a mistake."

He looked at Valmonde.

"We can't do anything for this man. It's been a long, hard ride down from Baton Rouge, Chief. We're going home to get cleaned up and rest. I'll check back with you tonight before we begin our usual patrol," he said as they left the morgue.

"See ya'll later then," Valmonde said as they mounted their horses and rode off.

Valmonde sighed.

If the Baron was in New Orleans, the city was in a world of hurt, especially since Hunter wasn't able to kill him after several encounters. Valmonde wondered just what kind of creature the Baron was and how Hunter and his friends planned to beat him if and when they did meet.

That afternoon, Lorena decided to drop in on Hannah Morii to see how she was handling the transformation. When she didn't see her in her customary place behind the counter, she called out her name. A few seconds later, Hannah emerged from the back room. She smiled at Lorena.

It was a weary smile at best.

"I came by to see how you are doing," Lorena said.

"I'm alright, I guess," Hannah said with a yawn.

"Any noticeable changes?" asked Lorena.

"Some. I'm incredibly energetic after sunset and sort of lethargic during the day. I've had to open the shop two hours later to compensate and I've noticed that bright sunlight seems to weaken me a little bit," Hannah said.

"It's only two weeks since I've turned you. You'll feel better and better as you progress. Just remember to wear dark glasses when you're outside during the day and to avoid too much direct exposure to bright sunlight," Lorena advised.

"You were right about having heightened senses," Hannah said. "I can see clearly in the darkest places and I can hear and smell things other people can't. I've also noticed that I have an enhanced sense of taste. All of my food tastes better."

"Have you had any cravings?" asked Lorena.

"None yet," Hannah replied. "How long before they start?"

"It was almost two full months before I started having them. Don't try to fight them. You will need human blood to survive and to complete the transformation. And those drinks they serve in the underground clubs won't be enough to satisfy you. You'll have to go out and kill someone," Lorena said. "Or find someone who will allow you to take enough blood from them to survive."

Hannah nodded.

"It's ironic, don't you think?" she asked.

Lorena smiled.

The idea that a person who had dedicated her life to hunting and killing vampires was now becoming a vampire. Hannah's situation was at least as ironic as her own.

Perhaps more so.

"Maybe when the urge strikes, I can hunt with you?" Hannah asked.

Lorena nodded. She leaned close and kissed her on the lips.

"Welcome to the sisterhood," she said. "We're heading for The Court of Two Sisters for dinner. Would you like to join us?"

"Sure. I haven't eaten anything since last night and I feel very hungry now," Hannah said as she slipped on a pair of dark glasses.

The Court was just down the street and it was shaded.

They sat down and ordered their meal. To Lorena's surprise, Hannah ordered three large courses and amazed her by devouring every last morsel. She also washed it down with several large, iced, mixed drinks. The drinks would have floored most people, but Hannah wasn't the least bit tipsy.

Lorena smiled.

"How do you feel after all those drinks?" she asked.

"Fine. I know I should be falling-down drunk by now, but I'm not even a little bit dizzy," Hannah replied.

"That's another benefit of being a vampire," Lorena explained. "We can never become intoxicated no matter how much alcohol we consume."

"I think I'm going to really enjoy this," Hannah said as she ordered another drink. "Normally, two drinks would do me in. Now that I know I can't get drunk, I'm just going to relax and have some fun."

They all laughed and raised their glasses.

After dinner, they escorted Hannah back to her store and headed for St. Charles to take the streetcar home. It was already past midnight. Lorena gave Hunter that "come hither" look he knew all too well.

"I'll be up in a few minutes. I have to finish my letter to the Cardinal first," he said.

Lorena responded by grabbing his shirt collar and pulling him close.

"Finish the letter tomorrow. The Cardinal can wait—but *I can't*," she said.

He laughed and let her lead him upstairs.

A week later, Hunter's letter arrived at the Vatican. It was handed to the Cardinal by his new aide during dinner by Fra Capella, who had taken over for the promoted—and departed—Bishop Riccardo O'Shea.

The Cardinal stopped eating to read it. It was brief as always. Hunter was a man of few words. The Cardinal smiled as he read.

"Went witch hunting in Baton Rouge. Finished with a barbecue. I have reason to suspect that the Baron is in New Orleans.----H."

The last sentence made the Cardinal sit up and take notice. He reread it and handed it to Capella.

"Put this in his file with the others," he instructed. "Have you sent the package?"

"Yes, Excellency. The money should reach New Orleans in another week," Capella assured him.

"Good. I want you to send word out to our other Slayers who are currently working in Europe. Ask them to dig up all the information they can on the Baron," the Cardinal said. "I want to know if there is any trace of him here."

Capella nodded and left.

The Cardinal stood and walked over to the window. He looked up at the gathering storm clouds and shook his head.

If Hunter suspects the Baron is in New Orleans, then he must be there. His instincts were seldom wrong, especially regarding such matters.

But why had the Baron gone to New Orleans?

There was much unfinished business between him and Hunter. Lorena, also. Did he go there to force that one, final showdown? If he did, then the Cardinal was more than confident that the Baron would come to a well-deserved end at the hands of Hunter and his friends.

Or was this yet another of the Baron's tiresome cat and mouse games? If so, then he certainly went very far out of his way to play with Hunter's mind. What could he hope to gain from such nonsense?

The Cardinal sighed.

He looked back at his half-eaten dinner and decided that he should leave whatever it was be lest it prove as deadly as a touch from the Baron.

The dream was vivid.

Far more vivid than most he'd had.

The images swirled and changed chaotically. They were in no particular order, yet they all fit together somehow, like the pieces of a jigsaw puzzle run amok.

He saw a knight in armor astride a coal black horse riding at the head of a large body of mounted warriors while a crowd cheered and threw roses on the path before them. Above the column fluttered a blood-red banner with a gold dragon. Behind the column plodded thousands of dirty, bloodied and chained men. Some wore turbans.

All looked like Turks.

This was the aftermath of a great victory.

The scene changed.

The same knight now sat at a table in the middle of the field, dining on platters of roasted venison, wild boar and fruit. As he sipped wine from a golden goblet he smiled as he watched his soldiers mercilessly impale each of the prisoners and stand them upright in the field. The air around the knight was filled with the screams and curses of dying men as their body weight caused them to slide slowly down the stakes.

Then two bright red eyes appeared above the field along with the blazing numerals 1462.

"Who are you?" asked a voice in the distance.

Hunter woke up shivering. Lorena watched as he got up and dressed to go out. As usual, she'd give him a ten minute head start. Then she'd follow him. He looked at her and smiled.

"I have to go out," he said.

"I know," she replied.

He walked down St. Charles and into the French Quarter. The streets were filled with the usual drunken locals and tourists that had spilled over from Bourbon Street. Hunter nodded at a few and stopped to chat with a young couple who had recently arrived from Europe. Then he continued on his way to the more quiet part of the Quarter. Lorena, he knew, was less than a block behind him.

Watching his back as always.

He reached St. Ann, turned the corner and walked toward Rampart. Less than a block later, the familiar swirling mist moved down the street toward him. He stopped and waited until it completely engulfed him. A second later, the familiar sight of the tall, dark woman in a white dress and blue scarf emerged from the mist and smiled at him.

"Good evening, Marie," he greeted.

"Good evening, Hunter," Madame Laveau replied. "I see that you've had another dream. A more *vivid* dream."

He nodded.

"It doesn't make any sense. I saw a man in armor, feasting while his soldiers impaled helpless prisoners on wooden poles and set them up like trees around him. I've never had such a dream before. It seemed horrific and strange—and somehow very familiar," he said.

"Do you *want* it to make sense?" she asked.

"I'm not sure. Part of me does. The other part is afraid of the answer," Hunter said. "The last few dreams didn't make sense to me. There was the one where—"

"You saw a man signing a contract with the Devil," Marie finished.

He stared at her.

"You know?" he asked.

"I know everything," she replied with her usual irritating smile.

"If that's true, then tell me—was *I* the one who signed that contract?" Hunter asked.

Before he even finished his question, both Maria Laveau and the mist were gone. Hunter laughed, then cursed under his breath. He looked behind him and smiled as Lorena approached.

"You saw?" he asked.

"All I saw was you standing in the street talking to yourself," she said. "The same as I see every time I follow you like this."

"What about Marie Laveau and the mist?" he asked. "Did you see that?"

"No, mon cher. I only saw you," Lorena replied. "Madame Laveau only shows herself to you and only when she wishes to."

'Then I'm not going mad?" he asked.

She laughed.

"You are no madder than you've always been," she assured him. "And I wouldn't have you any other way."

He put his arm around her.

"Let's go to the Dragon," he suggested.

The Dragon was the largest club on the famous vampire underground circuit. It, and several of the other vampire hangouts, was owned and operated by Tony LeFleur, the unofficial leader of the city's vampire community. The Dragon featured good food, strong drinks and a thriving dance/music venue. It was a favorite for vampires, wanna-bes and tourists who wanted to sample another side of New Orleans.

Hunter, Lorena and DuCassal were good friends with Tony and well-liked by the city's underground patrons.

Almost as soon as they walked in sat down at the bar, one of Inspector Valmonde's men, Sam, rushed in, spotted them and hurried over.

"What's up, Sam?" asked Hunter as he sipped his drink.

"The Chief sent me to find you. There's been a murder and he thinks it's right up your alley," Sam replied.

They followed Sam out to street where a familiar carriage waited.

"The Chief gave me his carriage. He wants me to bring you there in a hurry, too," Sam explain ed as they climbed aboard.

"Where are we going?" Hunter asked.

"St. Louis Number Two," Sam replied as he put the carriage in motion.

CHAPTER THREE:
The Witching Hour

Sam drove them to St. Louis Cemetery Number Two. When they stepped out, he led them to the crime scene which was in front of a crumbling vault that had an oak tree sprouting from it.

Valmonde nodded when they walked over.

"What do you have, Chief?" asked Hunter.

"Female, blond, about 20 years old. No I.D. yet," Valmonde replied.

"What's the cause of death?" asked Hunter.

"See for yourself," Valmonde said as he stepped aside.

There before them was a young, blond-haired woman staked to the ground by her wrists and ankles. She was completely naked and her chest and stomach area were covered with blood from the gaping wound in her chest. There was a makeshift altar on a flat stone next to her that had a single black candle in a silver cup. Both were in the center of a crudely drawn pentagram.

Hunter knelt down to examine the body. He took out his knife and gently poked around in the open chest wound. He looked up at Valmonde.

"Her heart's been removed. My guess is that's what's left of it on that altar. Whoever did this burned it as some sort of offering," he said.

"Offerin'? To who?" asked Valmonde.

"More like to *what*," Hunter said.

"Her lips are sewn shut. Let's find out why," he said as he cut the strings.

They watched as he pried her mouth open and reached inside. He pulled out what appeared to be a very large coin of some sort. It had odd-looking symbols on one side and the depiction of a strange, multi-armed being with a large, octopus-like head with tentacles coming from it. He stood up and showed it to the others.

"It's some sort of medallion or talisman," he said. "I've never seen anything like it."

"Me neither," DuCassal added. "What *is* that thing anyway?"

"Perhaps it's some sort of deity or demon?" Lorena suggested.

Hunter shrugged.

"We need to bring Minerva in on this," he said.

"I'm way ahead of you. I sent Lem over to fetch her an hour ago. That's her carriage comin' now," Valmonde said as he pointed up the street.

They watched as Minerva pulled up and climbed down from the driver's seat. She walked over to them and visibly blanched when she saw the victim.

"Oh, my dear Lord!" she cried.

"It *is* pretty disgustin'," Valmonde said.

"It's more than disgusting. It's *horrible!*" Minerva said as she looked at the body. "Is anything missing from her?"

"Whoever did this cut her heart out and burned it on that altar. They also put this in her mouth," Hunter said as he showed her the coin.

As soon as she saw it, Minerva shuddered.

"What do you think?" Valmonde asked.

"Let me look around a bit first. I've never seen anything like this in all my years in New Orleans," Minerva replied.

She looked the area over carefully. They saw her shake her head several times before she knelt down next to the body and said a quiet prayer. She then made several signs over the woman with her hands, sighed deeply and walked back to them.

"That was to put her soul to rest," she explained.

"What are we dealin' with, Minerva? Is this some sort of voodoo?" asked Valmonde.

She shook her head.

"This isn't voodoo, Leon. This is something much older and very, very dark," she said. "This poor child was ritually sacrificed to something evil. Something that demands a human life."

"You mean this is something Satanic?" asked Hunter.

"No. The Devil doesn't require human sacrifices. He just wants souls. This is something much older. Something to do with the Elder Gods," Minerva said. "I'm almost certain of that."

"Is this one of them?" asked Hunter as he held up the coin.

"I think so. I'll have to look in my books to be sure," Minerva said. "If I'm right, this ritual was part of an attempt to open the gate between their world and ours. Someone is trying to summon one of those gods."

"How do you know they haven't succeeded?" asked DuCassal.

"If they had, we'd all be kissing our asses good-bye right now. If even one of those things crosses over, it will be the end of everything as we know it. And what replaces it won't be pleasant," Minerva said.

"And just *who* are these Elder Gods?" asked Hunter.

"It's best you never know," Minerva replied. "Just be thankful that whoever did this didn't get it right. This was done by someone who managed to get several things wrong. If they hadn't, we'd all be dead now. So would they."

"You mean we're dealing with *amateurs*?" asked Lorena.

"Possibly. More likely, it's some sort of coven that's experimenting with something they don't truly understand," Minerva replied as they walked back to her carriage.

"Great! All sorts of things happen when people fool with something they know little about," Hunter said. "Most of them bad."

"Since they know they failed this time, I believe they'll try again. That means they'll try to sacrifice someone else soon. They'll have to do it before the last night of the full moon or the spell won't have a chance to work," Minerva said as she boarded the carriage.

"That gives us three more nights to find them," Hunter said as he looked up at the full, bright orb. "And we'll have to do it before they kill anyone else."

"I'll double the patrols," Valmonde said. "Especially in areas where pretty young woman hang out."

Hunter nodded.

"And we'll add an hour to our nightly rounds. We have to find these people before they accidentally get it right and bring the world to an end," he said.

"What? Again?" DuCassal moaned. "That's what brought about the Second Age."

"If the Elder Gods return to this world, there won't be a Third Age, Jean-Paul. There won't be anything but darkness and chaos until the end of time," Minerva warned. "I'll see you folks at the temple this evening."

They watched her drive off.

Hunter looked back at the body. Valmonde's men were just wrapping her in a blanket. Soon, the ambulance would arrive to take her to the morgue, where her family would be able to claim her.

"Just another night in New Orleans," he told himself.

That evening, they dropped by the Voodoo Temple on Chartres. Minerva was seated in her usual spot, sipping herbal tea. There were three cups and saucers and a plate of spice cookies on the table in front of her. She smiled at they sat down and helped themselves to the treats.

"Anything new?" Hunter asked.

"A little. I was able to identify the thing on the amulet. That is a depiction of the ruler of the Elder Gods," Minerva said.

"You mean Cthulhu?" asked DuCassal.

Minerva nodded.

"Tell me more about these Elder Gods," Hunter urged.

"A billion years ago, long before any human beings walked this Earth, it was a place of darkness and despair. A strange race occupied the universe. They were a dark, twisted people and they served even darker, more twisted gods. These were the gods of chaos and misery. Of destruction and death.

According to the legends handed down through the millennia, the Elder Race and their gods were driven from our universe after a long, bloody war and the "gate" was locked behind them to prevent their return. Supposedly, all knowledge of this was lost—until a writer named Lovecraft discovered a very ancient book. It was a Latin translation of an even older book and it told all about the Elder Gods. It also contained specific spells one could cast to open the gate and allow the Elder Gods to return to our world," Minerva said.

"I know that book. You're talking about the Necronomicon—the Book of Dead Names," Hunter said. "I thought every copy was destroyed centuries ago."

"So did I," Minerva said. "But I suspect that some copies still exist. Bear in mind that if they do, they are only translations of the original text and we all know that things are often lost in translations."

"So even if someone has a copy and is able to read the spells, it might not do him any good?" Lorena asked.

"Let's just say that the spell he casts may not do exactly what he expects it to do," Minerva said with a grin. "He may try to summon one of the Elder Gods and end up getting something even worse."

"What in Heaven's name could possible be worse than the Elder Gods?" Hunter asked.

"I don't even want to think about such things, Hunter," Minerva said. "But if that coven *does* have a copy of the Necronomicon, we'll have to find it and burn it before they can make use of it."

"This sounds worse by the second," DuCassal said.

"Never challenge worse, Jean-Paul," Hunter said. "It *always* surprises you."

New Orleans Municipal Hospital, five a.m.

The nurse at the station of the ward for terminal patients looked up when she heard the elevator doors open. She watched as a tall, rather handsome, middle-aged priest stepped out. He had a cross around his neck and a leather-bound Bible tucked in the crook of his left arm. The priest walked up to her and smiled.

"I am Father Gregory. I'm here to perform the last rites for one of your patients, but I have forgotten his name," he said.

"The only one we have on the terminal list is Jeffry Hammond. He's in room six just to the left," the nurse said.

The priest thanked her and walked down the hall. When he reached room six, he entered. Jeffry Hammond was lying on the bed and barely breathing. What breaths he did take were labored at best. The priest stood over him and smiled.

"I have come to ease your transition into the next life," he said as he reached out and laid a hand on Hammond's forehead.

Ten minutes later, the priest left the room. He stopped at the station to bid the nurse good day, then got on the elevator. The nurse didn't think anything of until she made her hourly check ten minutes later. When she entered the room, she saw that Hammond was completely covered by a white sheet.

"Maybe," she thought, "he expired while that priest was giving him his last rites. But why didn't he say anything when he left?"

She reached down and pulled the sheets back.

Then she screamed and screamed until several more hospital staffers raced into the room. One of them was the chief medical officer of the hospital. When he saw what was left of Jeffry Hammond, he turned to one of the aides.

"Go to Basin Street and tell Inspector Valmonde to get over here pronto," he ordered. "I'll have the orderlies take Hammond down to the morgue.

Valmonde, Sam, Hunter, Lorena and DuCassal arrived at the hospital an hour later. One of the aides escorted them down to the morgue so they could view the body as per the chief medical officer's orders. They were met there by the assistant coroner, Louis Turnbull, who shook their hands.

"This is damnedest thing I've ever seen, but it's kind of like that last one you sent over," Turnbull said as he led them to a series of cold storage drawers.

He opened the latch and pulled the drawer out to reveal a completely withered corpse. Hunter raised an eyebrow.

At that point, the nurse from the terminal ward entered.

"Thedra here was on duty when this happened," Valmonde said.

Hunter looked at her and smiled.

"Tell me everything you saw," he said.

The nurse told him all that occurred earlier that morning. Hunter listened quietly and nodded a few times.

"You say the last person to see him alive was a priest?" asked Hunter.

"That's right. And it wasn't Father Paul. I know him. This was a new priest. I never saw him before," the nurse answered.

"We'll stop by the Cathedral and speak to Paul. Maybe he can shed some light on this new priest," Hunter said. "But I have a feeling that the man who came to see him was no priest. Not by a longshot."

"The Baron?" asked Lorena.

Hunter nodded.

"Just what kind of vampire is this Baron?" asked DuCassal.

"The Baron isn't like any other vampire you've ever encountered, Jean-Paul," Hunter said. "He's a true vampire lord. He can sprout wings and fly. He can change his appearance at will and the usual weapons have no effect on him. I've shot him. Rammed a stake through his chest and even attempted to set him on fire. Each time, he simply laughed it off and escaped. The Baron is a bad one. Real bad."

"He's a *different* type of vampire," Lorena added. "While most of us need human blood to sustain our lives, he feeds off a person's life force. A single touch of his hand against bare flesh will live a person feeling feverish, weak and dizzy for several days. The symptoms mimic those of the flu, so the victim doesn't realize he's been attacked."

"And victims usually recover in two or three days," Hunter said.

"That seems rather harmless," DuCassal remarked.

"But it *isn't*. Each touch destroys a person's immune system and leaves him open to all sorts of viral infections. It also takes at least ten years off a person's life," Lorena explained. "It's a slower death, but death just the same.

"That's how he usually feeds. He prefers to remain undetected. When he's especially hungry or pissed off, he'll drain a person's entire life force, leaving nothing more than a dried corpse behind. If he decides to only take half a person's life force, that person becomes a vampire. That's what he did to me," she said.

"But you drink blood," DuCassal pointed out.

Lorena nodded.

"Only one person in every 100, 000 has the genetic makeup to become like the Baron," she said. "I am not one of them."

"Are you sure this is *his* work?" DuCassal asked as he looked down at the withered face on the table.

"It's either him or someone he turned," Hunter said. "The Baron is usually more subtle than this—unless, of course, he's trying to make a point."

"A point?" DuCassal asked.

"Yes. The Baron loves to play mind games. He'd relish the irony of hunting victims right under our noses here in the streets of New Orleans. It's like he's throwing it in our faces and daring us to do something about it," Hunter replied as he pulled the sheet back over the corpse.

"What can we do, Charles?" asked DuCassal as they left the morgue. "How do we find him? We don't even know what he looks like."

"We do what we always do and wait for the Baron to make his next move. Right now, we have a more urgent matter to take care of," Hunter said. "The Baron's not the only killer stalking the city now."

After they left the hospital, they decided to head for Jackson Square. The area in front of the Cathedral was crowded with street entertainers, artists, fortune tellers, musicians and tourists as usual. They made their way past the crowd and entered the Cathedral. Father Paul was up on a ladder adding a fresh coat of paint to the statue of St. Joseph when he heard the door open and shut. He climbed down and rushed over to greet them. Paul was the only "official" priest in New Orleans and he took the job because no one else wanted it.

"And to what do I owe the pleasure of your visit today, my friends?" he asked as they sat down on the steps of the altar.

Hunter told him what happened at the hospital. Paul looked surprised.

"A priest? Hell, Hunter. I'm the only priest in New Orleans as far as I know. If another one's in town, I have no idea who he might be. I know that he hasn't come to see *me* yet," Paul said.

"I doubt that you'd *want* a visit from this one," Hunter said.

Paul laughed.

"Any idea who it might be?" he asked.

"The Baron," Hunter said.

Paul shook his head. Hunter had told him all about his encounters with enigmatic vampire lord.

"You mean that vampire you've been chasing for the last decade or so??" he asked.

Hunter nodded.

"That'd be *my* guess," he replied.

"If it *is* him, what in Hell's he doing in New Orleans?" Paul asked.

"That's exactly what I intend to find out," Hunter replied.

They left the cathedral and walked over to Burgundy Street to allow Lorena to purchase something at her favorite boutique. While she shopped, Hunter and DuCassal browsed through some antique stores. They knew that Lorena would probably try several things on before she purchased them.

And that could take hours.

At four p.m., a short, white haired old woman left the shop in the middle of Burgundy Street. Before she took three steps, three young hoodlums accosted her and forcibly relieved her of her purse. While the woman yelled for help, they laughed and walked up the street.

DuCassal was walking down the street when heard the woman's cries. He spotted the four toughs as they crossed the street with the purse and stepped in front of them. They stopped. The largest of them sneered at him and handed the purse to the man next to him.

"I suggest that you return that purse and its contents to its rightful owner—if you know what's good for you," DuCassal said sternly.

"Yeah? And just how in Hell are you gonna make us do it?" the big man said as he crossed his arms over his chest.

DuCassal smiled.

He pulled aside his duster to reveal the holstered revolver at his hip. The toughs took one look at the weapon, turned and raced up the street. When they hit the next corner they stopped to see if he was chasing them. When they didn't see him, they relaxed and laughed.

"Man! That was close!" one said.

"Yeah," the big one said. "But we got away with the loot."

"I wouldn't say *that!*" came a voice from behind them.

They whirled around and stared as Hunter came at them with clenched fists. Before they could blink, he was on them and dealing out punishment from all directions. Ten seconds later, Hunter picked up the purse and walked back down the street, leaving the three toughs lying in a pool of blood, their bodies covered with bruises, scrapes and cuts and with a few of their bones broken.

"Jesus! Anybody get the number of that freight wagon that just hit us?" one moaned as he rolled over onto his back.

"Damn! Who on Earth was that guy anyway?" the big one said as he struggled to sit up and spat out two broken teeth.

"His name's Hunter and you men are lucky to be alive," said the officer who had just arrived on the scene.

He looked them over and laughed.

"I don't think I need to run you men in. I think Hunter taught you a lesson you won't soon forget. When you're able to, I recommend that you boys limp on home and stay there," he said.

"Yes, officer!" they all said at once.

Hunter walked over to the old woman and returned her purse. She gave him a warm hug and a big "Bless you, son!" then went about her shopping.

"I see those thieves ran into you, mon ami," DuCassal said with a grin.

"You mean *former* thieves, don't you?" Hunter said. "It'll be weeks before they recover from the beating I gave them."

"Perhaps they have been taught the error of their ways?" DuCassal asked.

"For now anyway," Hunter replied as they headed over to the boutique to see if Lorena was through with her shopping.

They arrived just as she stepped out of the store with two large shopping bags. She smiled.

"I'm sorry that I took so long," she said as she handed one of the bags to Hunter.

"That's alright. We managed to find something that occupied our time," Hunter said.

"Where are we going for dinner this evening?" she asked.

"How about Ralph and Kacoo's?" DuCassal suggested.

"You're one!" Hunter agreed.

CHAPTER FOUR:
When the Hunger Strikes

Hannah Morii was making her usual after sunset patrol of the Treme neighborhood. There were rumors of a vampire prowling the area and two young women had already turned up dead in Armstrong Park. With Hunter and his friends busy elsewhere, Hannah decided to go after this vampire herself.

The night was clear and moonless.

The streets of Treme seemed darker than usual, despite the street lamps and glowing night club signs.

She walked up North Villere to North Robertson and turned left at the cemetery. When she reached Iberville, she thought she heard a muffled, terrified gasp. Normally, she never would have heard anything this soft. But her senses were heightened now. She could even hear a dog whistle if she concentrated.

She stopped and looked around.

Then she followed the sound down to Marais. When she reached the middle of a block, she saw a tall, dark-haired man dressed in black attempting to sink his fangs into a frightened young woman he had trapped against a wall. Hannah strode over and tapped him on the shoulder. When the vampire turned to see who dared interrupt his meal, she punched him in the jaw with all of her strength.

Much to her surprise, the blow sent the vampire tumbling to the curb.

"Run!" she shouted at the girl just as the vampire leaped back to his feet and came after her.

This time, Hannah kicked him in the face and sent him sprawling. The vampire roared with rage and sprang at her. He moved so fast, she barely had a chance to dodge his outstretched hands. She attempted to punch him again. This time, he batted her fist aside and grabbed her by the throat.

Then he looked into her eyes and released his grip.

They spent the next few seconds staring at each other.

The vampire smiled.

"You're one of us!" he said. "You are like me!"

That's when Hannah realized that her transformation was complete. The vampire held out his hands.

"It is senseless for us to fight each other. Join with me and together, we'll feast on the human cattle that surround us," he offered.

"Never!" she said as she used the drop, draw and kill stroke with her katana.

The vampire never saw it coming and she astonished herself by being able to do it much faster than she had ever been able to before. She watched as his severed head bounced down the street and came to rest in the gutter. Then his body slowly dropped to the ground. Hannah sheathed her katana, pulled a wooden stake from her pouch, and rammed it through the vampire's heart. The heart exploded and showered her with blood. Some got on her lips and she found herself relishing every drop as she slowly licked it off. She retrieved the head, dropped it next to the body, doused them both with oil and set it ablaze. As the flames and smoke rose into the night sky, Hannah walked back to the French Quarter.

"I'm a vampire," she said. "But I'll never be like *him*!"

On the way to her shop, she began to feel hungry. The further she walked, the hungrier she grew. By the time she reached the shop, she was absolutely ravenous. But, she realized, she wasn't hungry for food.

It was more of a thirst.

That little taste of blood she'd had earlier had triggered something she was hoping to put off. Now she understood what Lorena went through.

What *every* vampire went through.

There was no sense fighting it. It would only grow stronger and stronger. So strong, that it might make her do something she never would dream of doing. She turned around and headed toward Basin Street.

Ten minutes later, she walked in on a semi-drowsy Valmonde. He yawned and stared at her.

"Hello, Hannah. What brings you out here at this hour?" he asked.

"I came to see what's on the menu tonight, Chief," she said. "Anyone out there you want real badly?"

He sat up and looked her in the eyes.

"You've been turned!" he said.

Hannah nodded.

He smiled and reached into his desk drawer. He took out a brown file and handed it to her. She opened it and read the information on a woman, age 42, with dark red hair, who was wanted for killing her infant daughter.

"That bitch ground that poor child up like hamburger and fed her to her dogs. Her husband came home just as the dogs started eatin' on her and tried to strangle the woman. She stabbed him in the chest and took off for parts unknown. He's still in the hospital and the doc says he might not make it," Valmonde explained. "I don't want her alive, either."

"Don't worry. She *won't* be after tonight," Hannah promised.

She handed the file back to him and left the station.

Valmonde shook his head.

With two vampires hunting down and killing them, the local criminals didn't stand a chance anymore.

Two blocks from the station, Hannah ran into Hunter and Lorena who were still making their nightly rounds. Lorena saw the look in Hannah's eyes.

She turned to Hunter.

"I'm going with Hannah for a midnight snack. Don't wait up," she said.

Hunter smiled and watched as they headed toward Canal Street. The hunger had finally struck Hannah and Lorena was going along with her to make sure she didn't let things get too far out of hand.

With Lorena guiding and teaching her, Hannah soon located their quarry. The woman was hiding in an abandoned building on the edge of the Lakeview District. The building was boarded up save for the back door and one upstairs window. Lorena watched while Hannah scaled the side of the structure like a spider and entered through the window.

Then she waited.

Several minutes later, a raggedy-looking body came tumbling from the open window. It landed almost at Lorena's feet. She turned her over and smiled at the two bite marks in the side of her neck. A minute later,

Hannah walked through the back door. She was wiping her lips with her sleeve.

"Nice work. How was it?" Lorena asked.

"I hesitated at first. I thought that I would only take a little from her. But when I tasted her blood rushing into my mouth, I just knew I had to take all of it. Considering the crime she committed, I don't feel the least bit guilty about this," Hannah replied. "Now what?"

"We return to the station and tell Valmonde where to find her body," Lorena said.

When they reported their kill, Valmonde smiled.

He reached into his desk, picked up an envelope filled with bills and handed it to Hannah. She stared at it.

"What's this?" she asked.

"The reward for huntin' her down. There's 2,500 Louisiana dollars in there and it's all yours," Valmonde explained.

Hannah smiled.

She opened the envelope, counted out 1200 dollars and handed it to Lorena.

"This is yours for teaching me how to track her down," she said. "I'm sorry I took all her blood."

"That's alright, Hannah. I'm not hungry tonight," Lorena assured her.

"That's too bad, miss, cause I've got a couple more folks I'd like you to find," Valmonde said.

"Who are they?" asked Lorena.

He handed her two wanted posters. One was a man named Jeb Smith who was wanted for strangling his mother to death. Another was Carl Marlowe who was wanted for grand theft and the shooting of store clerk in Old Metairie.

Lorena nodded.

"We haven't been able to find either one of them fellers, and we've been lookin' for them for weeks now," Valmonde said. "Are you sure you're not hungry?"

"Well, maybe I am a *little* hungry," Lorena said with a smile. "Care to join me, Hannah?"

"I'd love to," Hannah replied.

Valmonde watched them leave the station and laughed.

Lorena returned to the mansion just before eight a.m. and tossed two bundles of cash on the coffee table. Hunter looked at the money and smiled.

"I take it that last night's hunting went well?" he asked.

"It went very well. Hannah and I are well-satisfied now. We won't need to feed for several weeks," Lorena answered.

She pointed to the cash.

"That's 7,500 dollars," she said. "Hannah and I split it evenly. I think her transformation is going very well. I was worried at first, but she seems to be able to handle it."

"Let's hope she continues to do so," Hunter said. "How about brunch at the Court?"

"I'd love to. Give me a few minutes to shower," she said.

Hannah stared at herself in the mirror for a long time. She had finally crossed the line. She was no longer human, but something *better*. She was a true vampire now. She had tasted human blood twice in one night.

And she'd loved every last drop she swallowed.

The kills gave her a fantastic rush.

They were intoxicating.

Heady.

There was no sense of guilt.

Only pleasure and a delightful sense of euphoria.

She laughed and twirled around like a drunken ballerina.

"I'm a *vampire!*" she shouted.

CHAPTER FIVE:
Coven

The day after, Sam ran up to Hunter, Lorena and DuCassal just as they left Arnaud's. Hunter waited for the officer to catch his breath.

"What's up, Sam?" he asked.

"We found another sacrifice over in Number Three," Sam said. "The chief send me to fetch you."

"Lead on," Hunter said.

When they reached the cemetery, Sam led them over to a half-crumbling tomb on the far edge of the central section. Valmonde smiled when he saw them.

"Looks like our witch struck again," he said.

Hunter looked at the mangled, naked corpse. Again, it was a young woman, about 20 years old. She was staked out next to the tomb and naked. There was a huge gash in her chest and her throat was slit.

Deeply.

But what caught Hunter's attention most was the fact that her lips, which had been sewn shut like the last woman's, were torn and bloody and open wide as if she had been killed in mid-scream. He knelt down and examined her closely.

"This one still has her heart," he said. "And her mouth is wide open. Something interrupted the ceremony."

"But what? Nobody reported that they heard anythin'," Valmonde said. "In fact, the caretaker found this one."

Hunter probed the woman's mouth with his fingers and located another amulet. He tossed it to Valmonde.

"The same people did this," the Inspector said. "I wish we could find out who these bastards are."

"Let me try something," Lorena said.

They watched as she lay down beside the body and closed her eyes. After a few minutes, she saw herself surrounded by 12 people dressed in long black robes standing in a circle. A 13th figure, dressed in a dark gray robe, was kneeling over her with a large, heavy dagger held over his head. He was uttering some sort of spell or prayer. She watched as the figure plunged the dagger into her chest.. At that same instant, she opened her eyes, snapped out of her trance and screamed at the top of her lungs. The figure in gray slit her throat with the dagger to silence her and cursed in disgust.

A second figure standing behind him stared down at the body as it twitched its life away.

"Damn it, Lars! I thought you drugged her so this wouldn't happen," she said.

"I did. The drugs must have worn off. Anyway, the ritual is ruined now. Let's get out of here before anyone comes to investigate her final scream ," the one in gray replied.

Lorena watched them leave, then sat up.

"It worked. I wasn't sure that it would, but it worked," she said as Hunter helped her stand. "I saw and heard everything the victim did before she died. I was able to put myself in her place."

At that point, Minerva drove up in her carriage and hurried over to the site. She looked down at the victim and uttered a prayer to help her cross over. She looked at Lorena.

"Tell me what you saw, child," she urged.

Lorena told them everything. Minerva paced while she listened then shook her head.

"Are you sure she said Lars?" she asked.

"Positive. Why? Do you know him?" Lorena asked.

"If it's who I think it is, we're dealing with a true psychopath. But I'm sure he was sent to Angola years ago," Minerva said as they walked out of the cemetery.

"Got a last name so I can check?" Valmonde asked.

"I'm not sure what his last name is. But I know who can tell us," Minerva said.

"Who?" asked Hunter.

"Magdalena Vargas," Minerva said. "She runs a voodoo temple over on Treme."

"Take us there," Hunter said as they climbed into her carriage.

Magdalena Vargas was a tall, black haired beauty with a Latin accent. She was about 45 years old and a well-known practitioner of the healing arts. Her temple was quite smaller than Minerva's and filled with candles, incense sticks and other paraphernalia. She greeted them with a warm smile.

Minerva asked her about Lars' surname.

"That depends," Magdalena said. "Lars went by several surnames. The one he used most was Van Vorhees. He used to be a True Believer like us, but he gave it up years ago. Voodoo was too benign for his tastes. He was into power and mind control. For a few years, he was into Satanism and other, darker things. I heard he even sold his soul to the Devil to gain more personal power. I don't know what he's into anymore. I haven't spoken or written to him since he was sent to prison 16 years ago."

They thanked her and hurried back to the station with Valmonde. He immediately sent Sam down to the archives. A few minutes later, he returned and handed the Inspector a dusty-looking manila folder.

Valmonde opened it.

"Lars Van Vorhees, aka Lars Kempfner. Age 62. Sentenced to life without parole for the ritual sacrifice of a ten year old girl 16 years ago," he read. "That happened over in LaFayette Parish."

"Is he still in Angola?" asked Hunter.

"I'll have to write the warden and find out. Give me a few days," Valmonde said.

"In the meantime, have your men double their cemetery patrols. They may get lucky and bag this madman before he can kill anyone else," Hunter suggested.

"I already have," Valmonde assured him.

Three a.m.

Hannah Morii tossed and turned fitfully in her bed. She was awash in sweat and shaking all over. Anyone who didn't know her would swear she was going through some sort of drug withdrawal problem.

But this was much worse.

Despite what Lorena had told her, Hannah was feeling the hunger again—and less than three days since her first kill. She did her best to ignore the pangs at first. She even tried to keep them under control by having a few "cocktails" at the Dragon. The drinks had helped—but only for an hour or so.

Then the craving returned stronger than ever.

After hours of trying to fight it, she decided to give in.

She decided to follow her instincts.

And feed.

She threw on her hunting outfit, armed herself with the katana, and left the shop. Twenty minutes later, she walked into the Basin Street station and entered Valmonde's office. The Inspector was just about to leave for home when she sat down the edge of his desk and smiled.

"Do you have anyone you want me to take down, Chief?" she asked.

"As a matter of fact, I do," he said as he reached into his bottom drawer and pulled out a file.

Hannah opened it and read the description of the wanted criminal. Then she closed it and handed it back to him.

"I'll have him for you by sunrise," she said.

Valmonde watched her walk out and shook his head. Sam passed her on the way in.

"She out hunting again?" he asked.

"Yes," Valmonde replied.

"But she only hunted a couple of nights ago," Sam pointed out. "She can't be thirsty again so soon."

"She is, Sam. But that's fine by me. After tonight, there'll be one less killer on the streets of New Orleans and that's *always* a good thing. But I *am* a little concerned that Hannah might becomin' *too* fond of the taste of human blood."

Sam nodded.

"Just as long as she doesn't try to feed on any of us, eh, Chief?" he said.

Two nights later, the rich, full moon cast its light over a bizarre scene in the heart of the old cemetery. Thirteen robed figures, one of them in gray, stood in a circle around a young, unconscious woman who was naked and staked the ground. The people began to chant, low at first, while one of them lightly tapped on a small drum to provide the beat. As the chanting grew louder and louder, it happened to attract the attention of three police officers who were patrolling the cemetery. They rushed toward the voices with their pistols drawn.

Just as the one in gray was about to plunge the sinister, obsidian blade into the victim's chest, one of the officers shouted and fired a shot into the air. The one in gray stopped in mid stroke and vanished into the night while the rest of group scattered in all directions. The police gave chase and managed to grab three of the witches before they could escape. The rest fled into the night.

They went back to the woman and cut her free from the stakes. She was out cold from the drugs but otherwise fine. One of the cops pulled a robe off one of the witches and covered the woman with it.

While one cop waited at the side of the woman, the others dragged the witches to the Basin Street station and tossed them into the cell.

After an hour of questioning that went nowhere, Valmonde sent Sam over to get Hunter.

Two hours later, Hunter, Lorena and DuCassal arrived in a carriage. Sam took them downstairs to the cell.

Valmonde smiled.

"We bagged three of them. But they won't talk," he said.

"Leave them to me, Chief. When I'm finished, they'll sing like canaries," Lorena said as she removed her cloak and tossed it on a chair.

She walked over to the holding cell and studied the three, middle-aged woman seated on the bare floor.

"Her!" she said as she pointed to the one on the left.

Valmonde nodded.

Sam opened the cell and dragged the woman out by her arm. Then he slammed the cell shut and stepped aside to let Lorena do her thing.

"Who is Lars? Where is he hiding?" she demanded as she stared into the woman's eyes.

"Go to Hell!" the witch said.

"You first, bitch!" Lorena hissed as she bared her fangs and sank them into the witch's throat.

The ones in the cell leaped to their feet and screamed in terror as their friend twitched and moaned while Lorena sucked the life from her. When she was finished, she simply stepped back and allowed the now-deceased witch to drop to the floor.

She wiped the blood from her lips and stepped to the bars. Then she bared her fangs.

"You can either tell us what we want to know, or you can join your friend," she threatened.

The witches looked at each other, then nodded at Lorena.

"Who is Lars?" she asked.

"He's a warlock. He's the high priest of our coven," one of them said.

"How long has he been the high priest?" asked Lorena.

"About a month. That's when he formed the coven. We don't know where he came from or what his last name is," the second witch said.

"Where is he now?" asked Hunter.

"We have no idea. We don't have any direct contact with him. All the instructions from Lars come to us through Maggie. She sends us these cards two days before each mass telling us when and where to meet," the first witch said as she handed him a small, white card.

"And that's all we know," the witch said.

Hunter nodded.

He stuffed the card into his pocket and they left the holding area.

"Think they were tellin' the truth?" asked Valmonde.

"I'm sure they were. Neither of them wanted to be the next course in Lorena's meal," Hunter said.

"You sure can be ruthless at times, Miss," Valmonde said. "But I suppose you have to be under the circumstances."

"Especially when dealing with such ruthless people like them!" Lorena said.

"Now what, mes amis?" asked DuCassal.

"Now, we find out who Maggie is," Hunter said.

"Any ideas?" asked Lorena as they climbed into DuCassal's carriage.

"I have my suspicions," Hunter replied.

"Where to, Sir?" asked the driver.

"Take us to the Dragon, George. We'll find our own way back from there," DuCassal instructed.

When they walked in, Tony LeFleur waved at them from behind the bar. They waved back and sat down at their usual table near the large window. Tony came over bearing a tray of their favorite drinks, then sat with them.

"I heard the cops nabbed three members of that weird coven," he said. "Did you learn anything about them?"

"We know that the warlock in charge of them is named Lars and that they get their instructions on where and when to gather from someone named Maggie," Hunter replied.

"Lars Van Vorhees?" Tony asked.

"That's who we think he is," DuCassal said.

"Last I heard, he was in Angola for life—and no one ever gets out of there," Tony said. "I have no idea who Maggie might be, though."

"If you learn anything, you know where to find us," Hunter said.

Tony nodded.

"I'll send Heather over to take your order. It's on the house as usual," he said as he got up and slapped Hunter on the back.

Three days later, Hunter, Lorena and DuCassal were visiting Minerva at the temple when a perspiring Inspector Valmonde entered. He smiled and sat down at the table with them.

"I thought you might be here," he said. "I got a letter from the warden over at Angola you might want to have a look at."

He took the letter from his pocket and handed it to Hunter. Valmonde helped himself to a spice cake and sat back while Hunter read.

"According to this, Lars Van Vorhees was killed one month ago by two other inmates who were frightened that he was trying to put a hex on them," Hunter said. "When did those women say the coven was formed?"

"A month ago," Lorena reminded him.

"A week after that, they made their first sacrifice," DuCassal pointed out.

Hunter looked at Minerva.

"How close were Lars and Magdalena?" he asked.

"Real close. They were lovers for several years," Minerva replied.

"Does she ever go by the name of Maggie?" Hunter asked.

"Sometimes her friends call her that. I see where you're going with this and I don't like it," Minerva said.

"And I hope I'm wrong. Do you, by chance, have a sample of Magdalena's handwriting?" Hunter asked.

"As a matter of fact, I received an invitation to a wedding from her only last week. I'll get it," Minerva said as she walked back to her office.

She soon returned with a large white card and handed it to Hunter. Hunter pulled the card one of the witches had given Lorena from his pocket and held it up next to the invitation.

"What do you think, Chief?" he asked.

Valmonde looked the cards over carefully.

"I'd say that they were written by the same person," he said.

"Which means that Maggie and Magdalena are one and the same," Hunter said as he passed the cards to Minerva.

She shook her head.

"I'm forced to agree," she said.

"Now, the next question is: was Lars powerful enough to be able to work his magic from the grave?" Hunter asked.

"I'm sure he was," Minerva said. "I wouldn't put anything past that man—especially if got his hands on that book."

"Next question: who is this person who calls himself Lars? Is he flesh and blood or some kind of spirit?" Hunter asked.

"He could be either or both," Minerva hedged.

"Or has Magdalena been possessed by Lars in some way?" Lorena asked.

"If she has, then we have to find out if he took her over by force or she willingly let him do it. If it's the former, we have to find a way to exorcise him from her body. If it's the latter, then we'll have to use more drastic measures," Hunter said.

Minerva almost blanched at this statement. Hunter's more drastic measures usually meant that someone was going to be killed.

"Bring her to me, Hunter. I'll find out which one it is," she suggested. "After that, you can decide what to do."

He nodded.

"We'll bring her tonight. What time is good for you?" he asked.

"Around midnight. I do my best work at that time," Minerva said.

Hunter walked into the temple and saw Magdalena praying before an altar. He strode over and used his fingers to snuff out the candle in front of her. She turned, saw who it was and scowled.

"Hello, Maggie," Hunter said. "Or is it Lars?"

Taken aback, she stared at him. Then she laughed.

"It's neither. My name is Magdalena," she said. "Lars is dead."

Hunter smiled and dragged her to her feet.

"And only the warden of Angola and Valmonde knew that," he said. "Since you knew it, you're either part of a very elaborate hoax or you've been possessed by Lars' spirit. The question is, which is it?"

"That's a pretty wild accusation. Too bad you've no way of proving it," Magdalena said smugly.

"I don't have to prove it. *You* do," Hunter said as he stepped toward her.

She turned and went for the back door only to find her way blocked by Lorena and DuCassal. They both smiled at her.

"What are you going to do to me?" Magdalena asked.

"That's up to Minerva to decide. We're taking you to the temple so she can determine if you're possessed. If you are, she'll try to perform an exorcism. If it fails, I'll kill you on the spot so you won't be a threat to anyone else. If it succeeds and I find out that you willingly allowed Lars to possess you, I'll still kill you. But I do promise that I'll be far more merciful to you than your were to your victims," Hunter said as he grabbed her by the hair and forced her into the street.

They took her over to Chartres Street and dragged her into Minerva's temple. Minerva met them in the parlor. Hunter held Magdalena by the arms while Minerva put her hand on her forehead and stared into her eyes.

"She's possessed alright—just like you thought. Take her to the ceremonial chamber in back and tied her to a chair so she can't break free," she instructed.

Magdalena cursed and threatened them with everything short of legal action as Hunter forced her into a stiff-backed, heavy wooden chair and held her while DuCassal bound her with a rope that Minerva gave him.

Minerva then took out a bag of sea salt and proceeded to draw a circle around Magdalena. She then took out a vial of sacred oil and made the sign of the cross on her forehead.

The oil sizzled slightly.

Magdalena screamed as if she'd been scorched and struggled against her bounds. Minerva picked up her staff and held it above Magdalena's head while she chanted. Magdalena's face contorted into a hideous shape then slowly became that of a bearded man in his early 60s.

"Damn you, bitch!" he growled. "You have no power over me!"

"We'll see about that, Lars," Minerva said. "You were never a match for me in life so you know that you're no match for me dead!"

"Bring it on, Minerva! I'm ready for you this time!" Lars snarled defiantly.

Minerva turned to Hunter.

"Leave us. This might take a while," she said.

They waited in the parlor and sipped tea while they waited. They heard screams, moans and loud threatening curses come from the sanctuary. After an hour, Hunter rose and put on his hat.

"Let's get out of here for a while," he said.

"I'm with you. All this noise is making me crazy," Lorena said.

"Let's go over to Maggie's temple and search for that book," Hunter said.

They returned to Magdalena's temple and searched it from floor to ceiling for anything unusual. When they entered her bedroom, a blast of icy cold air rushed over them. Lorena and DuCassal looked at each other.

"That can't be a good sign," DuCassal said.

"I wonder what caused it?" Hunter mused as he looked around.

They spotted a trunk at the foot of her large, canopied bed. Hunter opened it. It was filled with gray robes, gold charms and a smaller wooden box with odd creatures carved into the lid. Hunter picked it up and felt a strange burst of power rush through his body.

It was a dark kind of power.

He put the box on the floor and opened it. Inside was a very ancient, heavy, leather bound tome with brass hinges. A strange, large headed, tentacled being was embossed on the cover. He reached down into the box to get it.

The moment he touched the tome, images of battles, fires and a man signing a contract with the Devil swirled through his mind. The images came at him like a strobe light. They were quick, sharp glimpses into various times, places and events. He dropped the book and slammed the lid shut.

He looked at Lorena.

"Is it the Necronomicon?" she asked.

"I don't know what that book is, but I do know that it's evil. It has to be destroyed before anyone else can get their hands on it," he said.

DuCassal picked up the box.

"I'll take it out into the courtyard and burn it. I'll meet you back at Minerva's when I'm finished," he said.

Hunter and Lorena headed back to Minerva's temple. DuCassal carried the wooden box down the back steps and into the courtyard. He placed it in the middle of the brick path and opened the box.

Almost immediately, his brain was besieged by strange, guttural voices chanting in a language he'd never heard before and couldn't understand. This was accompanied by a strange tingling sensation.

It was as if the book was trying to possess him in some manner.

He shook the feelings off as he doused both the box and the book with a vial of oil. Then he ignited it with a match and stepped back to watch.

As the flames slowly consumed the box, images of strange, twisted beings appeared briefly in the smoke amid a cacophony of cries and chants. The higher the flames rose, the lower the sounds grew.

DuCassal watched until the both the box and the book inside of it were reduced to ashes. When he was sure that both were destroyed, he doused the ashes with water from a nearby garden hose.

When Hunter and Lorena reached the temple, they immediately went into the sanctuary. Minerva was seated in a high-backed chair and fanning herself with an old silk fan. She had a whiskey bottle in her lap. Inside the bottle was a mandrake root and it was glowing ominously.

She smiled and held it up.

"I did it, Hunter. I trapped that bastard good. Maggie's all yours now," she said.

Hunter looked at Maggie who was still tied to the chair. She was badly bruised in several places and her lips were bleeding. She squinted up at him but said nothing.

"What did you learn?" he asked.

"She and Lars made a deal years before he went to prison that if he was about to die, she would allow him to possess her body to carry on his work—whatever that was—until he could find a suitable replacement body," Minerva said.

"So she was in cahoots with that madman?" DuCassal asked.

"She sure was. She had gone over to the dark side with him a long time ago. She just kept up the pretense of practicing voodoo so no one would suspect what she really worshipped," Minerva said.

"Power!" Hunter said with contempt.

"Exactly!" Minerva nodded.

"Why is she all bruised up like that?" asked DuCassal.

"I had to *beat* the Devil out of her—*literally*," Minerva said. "I had to make her physical body too weak and almost unconscious in order to draw Lars out and trap him in this bottle. Now all I have to do it throw him in the gulf and let the currents take him where they will."

Hunter untied Maggie and yanked her to her feet.

"What will you do to me?" she asked weakly.

He dragged her into the courtyard and forced her to kneel. He drew his revolver and placed it against her temple.

"You allowed Lars to use your body in order to perform those sacrifices. That makes you as guilty as he is. It may have been his will controlling your actions, but in the end, it was *you* who held the knife and *you* who murdered those girls. Putting you in prison is both dangerous and a waste of money. I can't take a chance on the possibility that you might one day escape," he said as he squeezed the trigger.

"I'll see you in Hell, Hunter!" Magdalena said as she closed her eyes.

The shot blew half her head to small, bloody fragments. Hunter kicked her to the ground, then doused her with oil and struck a match. Minerva and the others watched as he set her ablaze. Then, to everyone's surprise, the flames suddenly blew out and Magdalena's body vanished.

"What happened? Where'd she go?" asked an astonished DuCassal who had just arrived in time to witness it.

"She went to join Lars," Minerva said. "Their spirits are one, now."

"Can they come back?" asked Lorena.

"That, my child, remains to be seen," Minerva answered.

"If they do, I hope it won't be during our lifetime," Hunter said.

They joined Minerva in the parlor for some iced tea. DuCassal explained what he felt before he burned the book.

Minerva shook her head.

"At least that copy is no longer in the world," she said. "I wonder how many others are still floating around?"

"I'm not sure I want to know the answer to that, Minerva," Hunter said.

"Me neither!" DuCassal chimed in.

They lingered for another hour to talk and joke like they usually did. Afterward, they walked over to the Basin Street station and reported everything to Valmonde.

The Inspector shrugged.

"That's no skin off my nose. You did what you thought was right and that's good enough for me. What about the rest of that coven?" he asked.

"Just leave them to me and Hannah, Chief," Lorena said. "We'll track them down when we feel hungry."

Valmonde laughed.

"That's fine with me, Miss," he said. "As far as I'm concerned, they're all guilty of murder anyway. I'll put the word out that you'll be lookin' for them. Maybe a couple will decide to turn themselves in."

And they did.

Within a week after the word hit the streets, five of the would-be witches turned themselves in at the station, figuring it was best to trust their fate to the local justice system rather than be hunted down and killed by Lorena.

The other witches were never seen or heard from again.

Valmonde figured that they'd left Louisiana. As long as they were out of his jurisdiction, he didn't care where they went.

"Fear puts the wings of Mercury on many a person's feet," he said.

CHAPTER SIX:
Welcome to Slaughterville

Nine p.m.

The steamship, Savannah Queen, eased into the harbor of the Hostess City after a long, unexpectedly stormy voyage across the Atlantic. Normally, Savannah nights were clear and starlit.

This night, things were different.

The city was blanketed by a dense, pea-soup fog that lent a ghostly, almost otherworldly look to the ancient city.

It obscured the stately live oaks and ancient mansions. The only signs of light came from the city street lamps and they were barely able to penetrate the shroud.

Savannah was one of the oldest cities left in North America It's historic roots stretched all the way back to the early colonial period and it showed no signs of changing or going away.

Savannah was founded in 1733 of the First Age by British general James Oglethorpe who ingeniously designed the city around 24 interconnected squares. Each square was surrounded by homes, shops, city buildings and churches. The squares were common grounds where the original colonists cooked, washed clothes and basically hung out on those famous sultry summer nights.

It was originally a silk producing colony. Oglethorpe and his partners imported thousands of silk worms from Asia to seed the project. The colony did well at first, but a strange virus or blight struck early the next year and wiped out the silk worms.

The city then turned to producing cotton, sugar cane and rice.

By the time of the Revolution, Savannah had become the fourth largest city and seaport in the Americas and the wealthiest city in the South. It remained an important seaport almost to the end of the First Age.

During its long history, it survived epidemics, wars, fires and fierce storms. It even survived the Great Disaster. Each time, the city's inhabitants rebuilt it to make it look like it always had before. In this respect, they were much like the people of New Orleans and nearby Charleston.

The locals were proud of their city and its history. The people were hospitable, friendly, well-educated and more than a bit quirky. For example, they liked to boast that Savannah was the most haunted city on Earth. Just about every family owned a house or establishment that had at least one ghost. Anyone who didn't have a ghost in their house was considered a second-class citizen.

Savannahians also walked dead pets on invisible leashes, loved music, spicy food, drag queens and bawdy entertainment. They also gossiped about their neighbors and were very fond of throwing lavish parties and street festivals.

And they had made their city into an important seaport again.

Carmello and Riccardo O'Shea stood on the deck and watched as the lights of the city vainly attempted to penetrate the fog. The docks were little more than hazy shadows and they could barely make out the longshoremen as they hurried to prepare to receive the ship.

The O'Sheas were brothers.

They were also Slayers.

They were sent to Savannah by Cardinal Bertolieri at the request of the city's mayor. The Hostess City, usually known for its ancient Southern charm and historic sites, found itself besieged by a series of gruesome murders that their meager police force had been unable to solve.

In fact, several of the victims had been police officers.

The letter had reached the Vatican six weeks earlier. After what could generously be described as a rocky passage, the two Slayers had finally reached their destination.

It took another hour for the Savannah Queen to safely maneuver into its berth. It took another 30 minutes for the crew to lower the gangplank.

Carmello and Riccardo patiently waited alongside their black horses (which had made the crossing with them) until the rest of the passengers disembarked. They then bade farewell to the captain and crew and led their steeds down the gangplank and onto the pier.

The fog was everywhere now.

It was so thick, they barely saw the light from the carriage lantern as it slowly approached and drew to a stop. The window opened and a middle-aged man with long hair leaned out.

"Are you the Slayers we sent for?" he asked.

"Yes, we are," said Carmello. "Are you Mayor Toomey?"

"No. But if ya'll follow me, I'll take you to city hall," the man said.

"Is the fog always this bad here?" asked Riccardo.

"Hell, we rarely get fog here in Savannah. This is what you might call an anomaly," the man replied. "It started rolling into the city a few months ago. Now, we get it nearly every night when the humidity's too high—like now," the man said.

"Interesting," Carmello said as he climbed onto his horse.

Riccardo also mounted his steed.

"Tell me something, Mister.--?" he began.

"Martinez," the man replied. "Abel Martinez, at your service, Sirs," the man introduced himself.

"Which came first? The fog or the murders?" Riccardo asked.

"I guess they started about the same time. Why? You suppose there might be some connection?" Martinez replied.

"In our field, anything is possible," Riccardo said. "Take us to the mayor."

"Follow me and watch out. Our streets are kinda narrow sometimes and the lights can play tricks in this fog," Martinez said.

"Just what have we gotten ourselves into, Carmello?" Riccardo asked.

"We'll know more about that after we've talked with the mayor," Carmello answered.

A half hour later, they stopped in front of the old city hall on Bay Street. The building was six stories tall and topped with a cupola For such an ancient structure, Carmello remarked that it was very well preserved.

"This isn't the original," Martinez said as he led them inside. "It was rebuilt about 150 years ago after the first one burned down. The architect followed the original blueprints exactly," he said. "But he did make one good change. He added three more toilets."

A young man in a deputy's uniform ran up and took the reins of their horses as soon as they dismounted. He reached out and shook their hands.

"My name's Josh Brown," he said. "I'll take your horses over to the police stables. Don't worry about them none. They'll be well taken care of."

Martinez climbed out of the carriage.

"I'm supposed to take you up to the mayor's office. After you meet with the mayor and the sheriff, I'll take you over to your hotel. You'll be staying at the River Street Inn. That's one of the finest hotels in Savannah. You'll like it there," he said.

"Is it haunted?" Carmello asked.

"Of course it is. Everything's haunted in Savannah," Martinez said with a grin.

He led them upstairs to the mayor's office and knocked. A man with a deep Southern drawl called out for them to enter.

When they did, they were greeted by a large, broad-shouldered man wearing a six-pointed badge. He shook each of their hands as he introduced himself as Sheriff Bart O'Hara. A tall, thin man with white hair got up from behind the desk and shook their hands as well. He introduced himself as Mayor Ron Toomey. He introduced the slender, hawk-faced woman seated next to him as his wife, Elise. She just stared at the Slayers and said nothing.

When Carmello attempted to speak to her, she turned her nose up to indicate she thought he was beneath her notice. The mayor rankled at the obvious snub.

"That's no way to treat our guests, Elise. What kind of impression of Savannah will such a thing make on them?" he said.

"They're *your* guests, not mine. And I don't give a rat's ass what they think of Savannah," she shot back.

Then, with nose in the air, she strode out as if she were a queen dismissing unwashed peasants.

"Nice lady," Riccardo joked.

"That woman hates everyone and everything but herself. She especially hates me," Toomey said. "I'd divorce her but I'd end up giving her everything I've worked for my entire life."

"She makes the Wicked Witch of the West look like Mother Teresa," Carmello opined. "You have my condolences, Mayor."

"Thanks," Toomey said. "Savannah is a beautiful, ancient city inhabited by kind, friendly folks. My wife, of course, is the exception, so don't go by her. I've told everyone here to treat you men like family—which they'll do anyway. That's just natural for us. I've also asked them to help you in every way possible because you're here to save our fair city."

"Thanks. That's very good of you," Carmello said.

"We sure are glad to see you fellas," Toomey said. "Things around here have gotten out of control."

"So we've heard. How many people have been murdered so far?" asked Carmello.

"You mean *butchered*. Whatever's doing this doesn't leave much of them behind," O'Hara said.

"Amen to that!" Toomey said.

"Let's take it from another angle. What can you tell us about this fog?" Riccardo asked.

"The fog started rolling in about six months ago. That's when the killings started, too. The fog covers the whole city for a few hours. When it rolls out, we find another body in the street," O'Hara said.

"That definitely means there's a connection. Does the fog roll in every night?" Carmello asked.

"No. It never comes on rainy nights or when there's a thunderstorm. That's why folks here have been praying for rain each night," O'Hara replied.

"How are the victims killed?" asked Riccardo.

"They're torn to pieces. They look like a pack of wild animals attacked them. You'll be able to see for yourself once this fog lifts. I'm sure another body will turn up somewhere," O'Hara said.

"How many have been killed so far?" Carmello asked again.

"Ninety-three. Three of them were deputies of mine. Good men, too," O'Hara said.

"Any witnesses?" asked Riccardo.

"None. All the victims have been lone travelers. Nobody has seen what's in that fog and lived to tell about it," O'Hara said. "We told people to stay indoors while the fog is here, but not everyone listens. There's always somebody who just *has* to be outside for some reason and they usually end up dead."

"That's all we can tell you," Toomey said. "You men have had a long, hard journey. Go on over to your hotel and check in. If you need me, you know where to find me. I'm usually here most of the time for *obvious reasons*."

They left the city hall. Martinez was waiting outside the door. He led them over to his carriage and helped them on with their bags. Sheriff

O'Hara followed them to the hotel in his carriage. When they got out, he led them to the desk and watched as they signed in. Then he followed them up to their room.

"I noticed that both you men walk with a slight gimp," O'Hara said. "You hurt?"

"I was fitted with an artificial leg after a pack of raptors tore mine off about seven months ago," Carmello explained. "It's a very good replacement that never comes off and I can move very quickly when I need to."

"I was badly injured years ago while training to become a Slayer," Riccardo said. "But I'm very fast on my feed when I have to be."

"I suppose injuries go with the territory," O'Hara said.

"Injuries and death," Carmello replied. "The life of a Slayer is neither glamorous nor safe. But we fill a genuine need. We like to say that we stand guard between the shadows and the light. We're the first line of defense between the human race and the things that prey upon us."

"How many Slayers are there?" O'Hara asked.

"Not enough," Riccardo said as they opened the door to their suite. "Nobody wants the job and those few who do usually fail the training."

It was a fairly large suite with two queen-sized beds and a large sitting room with a balcony that overlooked River Street and the Savannah River.

"My wife picked this out. I hope it suits you," O'Hara said.

"This is perfect," Carmello said. "Thank her for us."

"You can thank her yourself. She told me to bring you over to our house for dinner and she won't take no for an answer. She said if I didn't bring you, she would beat me with a wooden spoon," O'Hara said.

Carmello laughed.

"When you put it that way, how could we refuse?" he said.

Maureen O'Hara was a plump, perky redhead with bright blue eyes and an outgoing, cheerful disposition. When her husband introduced her to their guests, she gushed noticeably and apologized repeatedly for the mess the house was in. Of course, it was spotless because she had spent the entire afternoon cleaning and dusting.

At dinner, which consisted of fried chicken, biscuits and gravy, black-eyed peas, salad and the best pecan pie either of the brothers had ever tasted, they were introduced to the O'Hara's teenaged daughters: 18-year-old Kate and 17-year-old Elizabeth.

Both girls bore a strong resemblance to their mother. Kate had Maureen's outgoing personality and wild sense of humor. Elizabeth was more easy-going like her father.

The girls and the Slayers hit it off immediately. So well, in fact, that their quiet little dinner lasted well past midnight. By then the fog had lifted and the brothers decided to walk the 12 blocks back to their hotel in order to get a better feel for the city at night.

Kate and Elizabeth accompanied them as far as Bay Street, then returned home where their father greeted them at the door.

"What do you think of our visitors?" he asked.

"I adore them!" Kate gushed. "They are like breath of fresh air compared to the men around here."

O'Hare looked at Elizabeth.

"What do you think, Liz?" he asked.

"I like Riccardo. I think he's real cute," she said softly.

He laughed.

"You girls play your cards right and you might be able to get them to marry you," he teased.

"I have *already* dealt the first hand, Daddy. Carmello just doesn't know it yet," Kate said as she batted her eyes.

Maureen giggled.

"That's the same way I bagged *you*, Bart. You have any regrets?" she asked.

"Not a single one, my love," he assured her.

Their Southern charms didn't go unappreciated. Riccardo and Carmello talked about the girls most of the night. Carmello even went so far as to admit that he was smitten with Kate.

"Be careful, Brother," Riccardo warned. "She's already set a trap for you."

"And I've already allowed myself to fall into it—as have *you*," Carmello said with a grin. "Elizabeth isn't as open about such things as Kate, but anyone can see that she's set her cap for you. Be careful or you'll have a ring on your finger before you know it."

"I guess we're both doomed then, aren't we?" Riccardo said.

"I think we are doomed—to marry those two lovely young woman and to settle down here in Savannah," Carmello said. "We've fallen victim to their Southern charms. Before we know it, we'll be waving the old Stars and Bars and toasting Robert E. Lee on his birthday."

"You say that as if it is a bad thing," Riccardo said.

They both laughed heartily at this for a long time.

Daybreak.

The rising sun burned away what little remained of the fog and brought a false sense of calm to the city. An hour later, a man who was out walking his dog happened upon the pitiful remains of a young woman in Reynolds Square and that false sense of calm was shattered once again.

O'Hara and the O'Sheas arrived at the scene a few minutes later. Riccardo looked at the pile of torn clothing, ripped flesh and blood and winced.

"That poor woman's been ripped to pieces. She looks like a pack of wild animals attacked her," he said as he walked around the remains.

"I can't tell who she is because there ain't much left of her," O'Hara said. "She's just like all the others we found."

While Carmello examined the body, Riccardo walked around the square. He stopped and pointed at the ground.

"I think you'd better have a look at this," he said.

They walked over and saw the large, deep, paw prints in the soft ground.

Carmello placed his foot next to the largest print. To his surprise, it was several inches longer and wider. He squatted down and checked the depth.

"That's far too large for a dog or wolf, but it's definitely canine," he said as he looked up at them.

"Any wolf that made this would have to weigh over 300 pounds. Some of these prints are nearly four inches deep," Riccardo said.

"And there are several. That means there was more than one creature. We may be dealing with an entire pack," Carmello said as he stood up and looked around.

"But a pack of *what?*" asked O'Hara.

"Is there an animal expert in Savannah? Or a natural history museum?" asked Carmello.

"No—but there is a museum up in Charleston. That's a two day ride from here," O'Hara said. "Or you can take the steamboat. One leaves here every morning at six. That would put you in Charleston around one in the afternoon."

"Then that's where we'll go. First, I need a bag of plaster of Paris and a roll of gauze. I need to make a cast of these prints," Carmello said.

"The hardware store is just up the street," O'Hara suggested.

Dawn.

Sheriff O'Hara drove the O'Shea brothers down to the dock in his carriage. When they got out, they saw an old, weather-beaten steamship moored to the dock with its gangplank lowered.

Carmello looked back at O'Hara.

"That's your boat," he said. "Don't let her looks fool you. The Charleston Belle is one of the best ships afloat. She's never missed her daily run, not even in a storm."

Carmello shook his hand.

"Thanks, Sheriff. We'll see you tonight," he said.

"I'll be here," O'Hara assured him. "I hope they can tell you something up there."

"Me, too," Carmello said.

The sheriff watched as they walked up the gangplank and waited until the Charleston Belle chugged up the river. It would take her 20 minutes to reach the open sea, then she'd hug the coastline all the way up to Charleston.

"Good luck," O'Hara said as he told the driver to take him back home.

Elise Toomey strode through the living room and scowled at her husband, Ron. He was sitting in his easy chair pretending to read the newspaper to avoid speaking to her. She snatched the paper from him and tossed it on the floor. Ron leaned back and puffed his pipe as he looked up at her.

"What's got your drawers in a bunch now?" he asked.

"Those men," she said.

"What about them?" he asked.

"How long are they going to stay here?" she asked.

"Until they find out who or what's behind all these killings and put an end to them. Why? Does their presence bother you for some reason?" he asked.

"I don't like them," she said.

"Hell, you don't like anybody. I'm surprised you can stand to look at yourself in the mirror without cussing," he said.

"I want them gone now!" she screamed.

"I don't. I asked them here to help us out and they are welcome to stay in Savannah as long as they like," he replied. "And there ain't a damned thing you can do about it."

In a fit of anger, she reached out and slapped the pipe from his lips. Ron walked over and picked it up along with the newspaper. Then he stepped right up to Elise and glared at her.

"Do that again and I'll punch you through that window," he warned.

She turned in a huff and stormed out of the room. Ron returned to his easy chair and shook his head.

"Nasty old bat! It's a good thing we never had any kids cause if they'd have turned out like *her* I'd have drowned them," he said as he opened the newspaper. "Her own mother told me not to marry her. I should've listened to her."

New Orleans eight a.m..

Sam rushed over to Hunter's house to tell him that yet another emaciated corpse had turned up. This one, a woman, was found in Jackson Square by a couple of street cleaners. She was seated on a park bench with her head down as if she were asleep. It's when one of the cleaners went over to wake her that they realized what happened.

Hunter, Lorena and DuCassal arrived at the Square an hour later and made their way through a large crown of nosy tourists and locals. Valmonde and two of his men were standing guard over the body.

The Inspector nodded when they walked over to him.

"Looks like he got another one," Valmonde said.

Hunter knelt and looked into the woman's withered face. There wasn't a drop if moisture in her.

"This is *his* work alright," he said as he stood and looked around. "And he could be watching us right now."

"Don't you know what he looks like?" asked Sam.

"Of course I do. I know his face better than I know my own. But the Baron can alter his appearance at will. He can make himself look different so he can easily blend into any crowd. He can even become a woman. That's why you never know if he's around," Hunter explained.

"Whoever this fella is, he's sure keepin' busy," Valmonde said. "Does he need to kill so often?"

"No. Usually he just steals a little bit of energy from people he touches and leaves them feeling like they've caught the flu. He only kills like this to make a point," Hunter said.

"And just what point is tryin' to make now?" asked Valmonde.

"He's telling us that he's here," Hunter replied. "*If* the killer *is* the Baron. He's not the only vampire that feeds off human life forces. But such a thing is very rare."

"How rare?" asked Sam.

"Maybe one in every 5,000," Lorena replied. "It's hard to say. The Baron is the only one of his kind that I've ever met."

"One in every 5,000? Just how many vampires *are* there?" asked Valmonde.

"Far more than you think," Hunter said. "Most of them are like the ones who frequent the underground clubs here. They get their blood from willing donors in small amounts. It's enough to sustain them. Maybe one or two percent actually kill humans to survive because they need massive infusions of blood about once or twice each month."

Valmonde looked at Lorena.

She nodded.

"At least you don't kill anybody who doesn't need to be killed," he said.

"When I was turned, I vowed to use my abilities to help rid the world of vampires and vicious criminals," she said.

"And you've been more than a blessin' to this city, Miss," Valmonde assured her.

"Well, I do what I can," she said modestly.

"You and Hannah Morii," Valmonde said. "She tracked down two of them witches last night and left their bodies at the gate of St. Louis Number Three. She came by to collect the bounty just before sunrise."

"Hannah's feeding again? It's only been a few days since her last kill," Lorena remarked.

"She must have gotten hungry again," Hunter said. "Those early urges are nearly impossible to control. You said so yourself."

"I know. I guess I'm just worried about her," Lorena said. "I didn't expect her to feed again so soon."

Valmonde looked at her.

"Is somethin' wrong?" he asked.

Lorena shook her head.

"I don't think so, Chief," she said.

"Now, about this Baron—how are you goin' to find him?" Valmonde asked.

"We can't. The next move is up to him. We'll just have to wait until he makes it and try to react in time," Hunter replied.

"One can only find the Baron when he *wishes* to be found," Lorena added. "And he rarely tips his hand."

"He sounds like a real son of bitch," Valmonde said.

"He *is*," Hunter assured him with a smile.

Longue Vue, nine a.m.

Deloreon walked through the open front doors of the crumbling mansion. He stopped and looked around at the debris-littered entry hall and tall, paneless windows that flanked the front doors. A few small, black bats fluttered overhead, giving the ancient mansion a downright Gothic look.

The once grand home was deserted now. Its last occupant was the would-be vampire lord named Van Helsing. Then Hunter learned where he was and dispatched him.

Deloreon had not come to Longue Vue to sightsee. He came because he was summoned.

He was newly arrived in New Orleans. He had not yet made his first kill when the envelope appeared in his mailbox.

He knew his summoner by reputation only. That was enough to draw him to Longue Vue.

"You are precisely on time. I like that quality in my assistants," a man with a heavy Eastern European accent sad as he entered the room.

"The Baron, I presume?" Deloreon asked almost deferentially.

"In the flesh. I suppose you are wondering why I've asked you come here?" the Baron replied.

"Let us say that you have caught my attention," Deloreon replied.

"I want you to perform a small favor for me. Something that will catch the attention of a certain Slayer and his companions," the Baron said.

"Hunter?" Deloreon asked.

The Baron nodded.

Deloreon laughed.

"I've heard of him. Are you sure you *want* to get his attention?" he asked.

"I'm positive. This small favor will also help you, er, get your feet wet, so to speak. It will be your introduction to the people of New Orleans," the Baron replied with an almost evil smirk.

"What if I refuse?" Deloreon asked.

"In that case, your stay in New Orleans will be quite brief," the Baron warned. "I would do this myself, but I think it will be more interesting this way."

Deloreon took a deep breath and exhaled.

Going against the Baron would be suicidal at best.

"What will you have me do?" he asked.

Charleston, one p.m.

Charleston was a smaller, older city on the southern tip of a peninsula. As the steamship entered the harbor, it chugged past the crumbling ruins of an ancient brick fortress on a small, rocky island.

An older man standing next to Carmello and Riccardo on the deck pointed it out to them.

"That's old Fort Sumter. Back in the First Age, it was the scene of three long sieges. The last one came right near the end of the First Age and the invaders just about leveled the place. After the defenders retreated into the city, the invaders followed them and put Charleston to the torch," he explained.

"So the city was destroyed?" asked Carmello.

"Almost. The survivors fled into the swamps to the north and waited for the invaders to leave. When they did, the people returned and rebuilt Charleston. They made it look just like it always has because that's the way they like it," the man said.

"I notice that the tallest structures seem to be church steeples," Riccardo observed.

"That's because of an ancient city ordinance that states that no structure of any kind, either privately owned, business or government shall be taller than the tallest steeple because all things must remain under God," the man said.

Carmello smiled.

"I like that," he said.

"What brings you men to Charleston?" the man queried.

"We're going to visit the Natural History Museum. Can you tell us how to get there?" said Riccardo.

"I sure can. The boat will dock at that fancy-looking terminal up ahead. When you disembark, leave the terminal and turn left. The museum is about a half-mile down that street. You can't miss it," the man said.

They thanked him and watched as the steamboat slid smoothly into the terminal. They disembarked and followed the directions the man had given them. Less than ten minutes later, they found themselves standing before a large, brick and concrete structure that resembled an ancient Greek temple.

The museum covered an entire city block and stood two stories tall. It had tall, narrow glass windows and the front entrance was a ten foot tall bronze, double door. They entered and found themselves in a huge atrium surrounded by the reconstructed skeletons on long-extinct animals.

"Impressive!" Carmello remarked as he stared into the gaping jaws of an allosaurus staring down out them with its jaws wide open.

"Very!" Riccardo agreed.

"I'm glad you like it," came a voice from behind them.

They turned and saw a tall man in a white suit leaning on a cane. He smiled and extended his hand.

They shook it and introduced themselves.

"I'm David Allison Jourdan. I'm the curator here," the man said. "Welcome to the Charleston Museum of Natural History."

Jourdan was a pleasant natured man with a disarming smile. He had short white hair and matching goatee and mustache and spoke with a smooth South Carolina drawl. The museum had been his creation.

The fulfillment of a dream.

At the age of 25, he used his family's vast wealth to purchase and renovate the abandoned Port Authority building. Then he and his team of "raiders" as he called them, set about stocking it with exhibits that they rescued from abandoned museums around the world. Jourdan was also the curator of the Charleston History Museum and headed the local preservation society.

There was little he didn't know about ancient animals.

Carmello explained why they had come.

"Can I see the casts you made?" Jourdan asked.

Riccardo set the briefcase down on a nearby bench, opened it and carefully unwrapped the cast he had made. He handed it to Jourdan who held it up to examine it.

"It's most definitely canine in origin," he declared. "But this didn't come from any modern day animal."

He led them to a back room. Inside were rows of glass display cases that contained small scale models of various canine creatures. Alongside each was a life-sized cast of the animal's paw print.

Jourdan walked over to the case and held the cast up next to one print after another. After a while, he shook his head.

"That rules out modern canines. The closest I can get is a hyena—and this is far too large for that," he said.

"Any ideas what made it?" asked Riccardo.

Jourdan examined the cast in the light beaming through a window.

"Judging by the size and depth of this, I'd estimate that the creature that made it stands about eight feet tall at the shoulders and weighs around 800 pounds," he said.

"No living wolf is *that* big," Carmello said.

"True. But one such creature did indeed exist thousands of years ago. It was called a dire wolf or aardwolf. They were the ancestors of the modern wolves, highly intelligent, carnivorous and they hunted in packs. They were large and strong enough to bring down a mammoth. Besides the saber toothed tiger, they were the top predator of their time," Jourdan replied.

"Aren't they extinct?" asked Carmello.

Jourdan nodded.

"They've been extinct since the end of the Ice Age, yet the evidence you've shown me would indicate that they've somehow made a comeback," he said. "But the only way they could do that would be if someone genetically engineered it."

"That's impossible," Riccardo said.

"I don't know. Our friends in Opus Dei managed to resurrect the raptor. This could be another one their experiments run amok," Carmello said.

"But what of the fog? That suggests there's a decidedly supernatural element rather than scientific," Riccardo asked.

"Fog?" Jourdan asked.

They told him all about the strange series of murders that were plaguing Savannah. Jourdan listened intently and nodded when they'd finished.

"The events in Savannah have all the elements of an ancient folk tale. Ever hear of the Wild Huntsman?" Jourdan asked.

"Yes. Isn't that an old Scandinavian legend?" asked Carmello.

"Actually, it pops up in several cultures. They all have similarities in that the Wild Huntsman is described as a large, dark man astride a coal black horse. The Huntsman is dressed in either bearskins, wolf hides, leather or a combination of all three. He wears a helmet that's decorated with large deer antlers, and has a black beard and hair. Some legends say the antlers actually grow from the sides of his head. He is accompanied by a pack of up to a dozen very large, very primitive types of wolves with fiery red eyes. And he announces his arrival and the start of the Wild Hunt by blowing on a ram's horn.

It's said that he and his pack emerge from dense fogs. The fogs surround his intended prey and actually transports them into a dark, terrifying looking, barren wasteland of twisted trees and marshes. When the Huntsman bags his prey, he blows the horn three times, then vanishes," Jourdan explained. "The Huntsman never gives up until he bags his prey. And he can't be killed."

"Wow!" Riccardo said.

"That fits into what's happening in Savannah," Carmello said thoughtfully. "But it *is* only a legend."

"A wiser man once said that all legends and myths have some basis in fact," Jourdan said with a smile. "Who is to say what's real or isn't? The only way to find out if the Wild Huntsman is running loose in Savannah is to see him yourself."

"But in order for the Huntsman and his pack to cross into our world, he would have had to be *summoned*. Who in their right mind would summon him from the underworld?" asked Riccardo.

"Someone who really has it in for some people in Savannah. Someone who despises the city and its people for some reason," Carmello conjectured.

"Maybe he summoned the Huntsman to get rid of a specific person without realizing that he couldn't control him?" Riccardo suggested.

"This gets worse," Jourdan said. "Now that Huntsman has been summoned, he will continue to terrorize the people of Savannah until his summoner has been killed or you can find another way to send him back to the underworld."

"Good luck with that!" Carmello said with a grin. "We'll let you know how that works out for us."

"It can be done," Jourdan said. "I just can't tell you how to go about it."

"Why not?" asked Riccardo.

"Because I don't know," Jourdan replied.

They laughed and thanked him for his trouble. He invited them to come by again so he could show them around the museum and the city itself. An hour later, they were on the Charleston Belle for the return trip to Savannah.

O'Hara met them at the dock in his carriage and took them back to the River Street Inn so they could shower and get a good night's rest.

The next morning, Kate and Liz pulled up in front of the hotel in their father's carriage just as Carmello and Riccardo walked out. They smiled when the say the girls and walked over to them.

"We thought we'd take ya'll on a tour of the city. I hope you don't mind?" Kate said. "After that, ya'll can take us out to dinner at the Olde Pink House. It's the best restaurant in Savannah."

"We'd be delighted," Carmello said as he climbed aboard and sat down beside her.

Riccardo got in next to Liz.

"It's nice of your father to let us have his carriage for the day," he said.

"Oh, he doesn't know about it—yet," Kate said with a smile. "But he will when he realizes that he'll have to walk to work."

"Doesn't the driver work for your father?" asked Carmello.

"Usually. I gave him a hundred dollars to be our chauffer for the day," Kate replied. "And in case you're wondering, our Mama approved of this—so Daddy won't have anything to say about it."

They all laughed and took off down River Street.

They spent the day riding all over the city and walked along the snow-white sandy beaches of Tybee Island.

They talked.

They joked.

They laughed.

And the girls slowly but surely drew the O'Sheas into their tender trap, albeit they went willingly.

When Maureen told her husband why he had to walk to work that morning, Bart laughed.

"Those fellas may be Slayers, but you can bet your bottom dollar that they've never gone up against anyone like our two girls. Hell, they'll be at the altar before they ever know what's hit them," he said.

"I think it would be nice to have a couple of Slayers in the family. Don't you?" Maureen said.

Bart just laughed.

It's not like he'd have any say in the matter anyway.

New Orleans, ten p.m.

Hannah Morii walked into the Dragon and sat down at the bar. Tony LeFleur was behind the bar while his usual bartender took a break. He walked over to greeted Hannah.

"What'll you have?" he asked.

"A pint of your best—and I don't care what type it is," Hannah said.

"You want it mixed or neat?" Tony asked.

"Neat," she replied. "Chilled if possible."

"No problem," he said.

He went down to the other end of the bar and poured the dark red liquid into a tall chilled glass. He brought it back to Hannah and placed it in front of her on a cardboard coaster. She gulped it down without saying a word, then put the empty mug down on the bar and wiped her lips with a napkin.

"Thanks. I feel much better now," she said.

"Got the craving again?" Tony asked.

"Yes. They hit me when I least expect it. Did you have to go through this when you were turned?" Hannah asked.

"To tell you the truth, that was so long ago I can't remember. How often do you get them?" Tony replied.

"Every other day. It's like my body needs more and more blood each time. This is one Hell of an adjustment period," she said. "Let me have another—this time, I want your special sangria."

"Coming right up," Tony said as he made a mental note to discuss Hannah's problems with Lorena when she and Hunter stopped by that night."

CHAPTER SEVEN:
The Aswang

Mardi Gras Indians are tall, muscular Black men who wear costumes made of brightly colored, elaborate feathers, beads, necklaces, ankle bells and other accoutrements. They originally started out as entertainers and marchers in the annual Zulu celebrations. Now, they are sought after for all sorts of parties and festivals.

And they command high fees for their services.

Shem Champion was arguably the best of the Mardi Gras Indians. He stood six feet eight inches tall, was dark skinned and incredibly well built. He was so well-liked and known that he'd been elected to serve as King Zulu for the last eight Mardi Gras. It was a role he really enjoyed playing, too.

Shem was strutting his stuff at the annual Oyster Fest on the waterfront and having his usual grand old time wowing the mostly inebriated spectators with his acrobatic moves and fire eating abilities.

At the height of the festivities, Shem climbed onto the wooden platform to do his finishing act while the huge crowd stomped their feet and cheered. As soon as he reached the top of the platform and stretched out his arms. He was snatched into the air by a huge, shadowy form that came from out of nowhere.

As the people gaped in shocked disbelief, Shem struggled to break free of his captor. But it was to no avail. Shem was lifted a hundred feet off the platform and spirited away into the night, cursing at the top of his lungs the entire time.

Hunter, Lorena and DuCassal, who happened to be in the crowd, gave chase from the ground as far as they could. But Shem had already completely vanished along with his captor.

They walked along the waterfront for another mile or two, then gave up the chase. Shem was nowhere to be found.

Hunter cursed loudly as he kicked a tin can into the water.

"What in Hell was *that*?" asked DuCassal. "It looked like a gigantic bat!"

"That was the Baron," Hunter replied.

They headed back to the festival to continue their patrol.

The crowd remained silent until the next group of entertainers came out to perform and the party started up again. By midnight, most of the revelers had completely forgotten the bizarre incident.

By the next morning, most of them forgot they were even at the festival.

The next morning, Hunter, Lorena and DuCassal were discussing the situation at the Basin Street station when Sam walked in with the Times-Picayune and laid it on the desk. The banner headline read:

MARDIS GRAS INDIAN ABDUCTED FROM FESTIVAL

Valmonde looked at the headline.

"Any idea who did this?" he asked.

"I have my suspicions," Hunter replied.

"That Baron fella?" Valmonde asked.

Hunter nodded.

"He's done this several times before. Usually, he does it to strike fear into a local population. I doubt that's his motive this time," he said.

"You figure he did this to send a message?" asked Sam.

"I'd say that's a very strong possibility," Hunter answered. "He's letting us know that he's here in New Orleans and he's daring us to do something about it."

"Can you?" asked Valmonde.

"Yes," Hunter assured him. "But *he* has to provide us with the opportunity Right now, we have no idea where he is or what he looks like. The ball is in *his* court."

"That sucks a big one," Valmonde remarked.

"Yes, it does," Hunter agreed.

"What about Shem? Think he'll turn up?" Valmonde asked.

"Eventually," Hunter replied with a smirk that sent a shiver up Valmonde's back.

The smirk told him that when Shem did show up, he wouldn't exactly be a pretty sight.

"How many folks has this Baron killed?" he asked.

Hunter shrugged.

"He's been around for centuries. His victims probably number in the *thousands* by now," he said.

"That's quite a resume," Valmonde said.

"I'll say it is. If it is the Baron, he came here for a specific reason. Sooner or later, he'll tell us what that is," Hunter said.

He picked up his hat and they headed for the door. Valmonde walked out with them and noticed it was raining.

"A typical mornin' in New Orleans," he said as he looked skyward.

Hunter nodded.

"We're going to breakfast. Let us know when Shem turns up," he said.

The next morning, Shem's shriveled body was found lying at the base of Andrew Jackson's statue in the Square. As soon as Valmonde received the news, he sent Sam to get Hunter, Lorena and DuCassal. They met him in the Square an hour later and had to fight their way through the crowd to get to the statue.

Shem's corpse looked as if it had been drying in a kiln for a thousand years. Hunter shook his head sadly. Shem had been an acquaintance of his for a few months and his murder angered him.

"That's four in three weeks," he said as they walked out of the Square.

"The Baron is gorging," Lorena remarked.

"No. He's *murdering*. He's tossed down the gauntlet—and it's a challenge we have to accept," Hunter said.

"And we will, of course," DuCassal said.

"Of course," Hunter agreed.

They walked down to the Hannah's emporium to see how she was doing. When they walked in, she greeted them at the door with her usual smile.

"Those throwing darts you ordered came in last night," she said as she led him to a shelf.

She reached up and took down a small wooden box, which she handed to Hunter. He opened the lid and nodded.

"These will do nicely," he said. "How much do I owe you?"

"One hundred," Hannah said. "You can fit them with exploding caps, too."

"That's why I ordered them. I have a feeling they'll come in handy soon," Hunter said as he took two bills from his wallet and passed them to her.

"The Baron?" she asked.

He nodded.

"How are *you* holding up?" Lorena asked.

Hannah smiled.

"I feel fine now. I haven't felt the urge for a few days," she said. "How often do they come?"

"Once or twice each month," Lorena said.

"I thought this would really be a moral problem for me at first. Since I've made my first kill, the idea doesn't bother me in the least," Hannah said almost too cheerfully for Lorena's taste. "How did you handle it at first?"

"About the same as you," Lorena replied. "You just have to kill only when you need to and only kill those who need to be killed. Then everything will be fine."

"I heard about poor Shem," Hannah said sadly. "I've known him for years. He was a good man."

"I'll miss him, too," DuCassal said. "He owed me $25."

Hunter laughed.

"Good luck collecting it now," he said.

"I'd rather that Shem still be with us than have the money," DuCassal said. "Hell, I have far more of *that* than I'll ever need anyway."

At that very moment in a two story house on Euterpe, young Peggy Sandford went down into the cellar and picked up the axe her father, Fred, had used that morning to chop some firewood. She walked back up to the living room where her father was seated in a large, overstuffed chair.

He was busy reading the newspaper and didn't notice that Peggy had crept up behind him until she buried the blade of the axe in his skull. The sound of him hitting the floor brought Peggy's mother, Molly, running from the kitchen.

The first thing she saw was her husband lying in a pool of blood. When she screamed and turned away, she happened to see her daughter standing in front of her with the bloody axe raised high.

Seconds later, Molly's headless corpse thudded to the floor and mingled her blood with that of her husband.

Peggy dropped the axe.

She walked back upstairs to her parents' bedroom and opened the balcony doors. After taking a brief look up at the mid afternoon sun, she stepped onto the rail, spread her arms out and threw herself into the courtyard below.

Neighbors heard Peggy hit the pavement and hurried over to see what happened. One of them hurried to the police station on Basin Street and told Valmonde what they found. An hour later, he and Sam were at the Sandford home going over the gruesome crime scene.

Valmonde shook his head.

"Looks like we have us a murder-suicide, Sam," he said. "Peggy went off the deep end for some reason and murdered her folks. Then, when she realized what she done, she killed herself out of guilt."

"I think you're right, Chief. But what would make Peggy do such a thing? I thought she was a happy young lady. She was going to the best private school in the city and her parents treated her like a princess," Sam said.

"There's no tellin' what makes folks go crazy like that," Valmonde said. "I'll have the ambulance come over and fetch the bodies. You go and tell Fred's brother, Earl, what happened."

"Earl lives over in LaFayette," Sam reminded him.

"Right. I'll have to send him a letter," Valmonde said.

Before the letter reached LaFayette, the city was rocked by another bloody crime.

Millie Burgess, a plump, middle-aged woman who'd been married to Calvin for the last 25 years, was standing at the kitchen counter chopping vegetables for the evening meal while her husband was setting the table. Millie suddenly turned, walked up to Calvin, and proceeded to stab him to death.

She plunged the knife into him 25 times.

When she was positive the deed was done, Millie dropped the knife, went upstairs to the bedroom and threw herself from the balcony.

Valmonde and Sam hurried over as soon as they received the news. Calvin had been stabbed so many times that his chest and face looked like hamburger and the kitchen floor was slick with blood.

Millie had done a header from the balcony, so there wasn't much left of her skull and her brains were splattered all over the courtyard.

Valmonde shook his head.

"Another murder suicide. That's two in three days," he said.

"They're so much alike, this just can't be a coincidence, Chief," Sam said.

"I don't think so either, Sam. Go and fetch Hunter. I think we need to tell him about this," Valmonde said.

A half hour later, Hunter, Lorena and DuCassal stepped out of the carriage and walked over to Valmonde who was seated on the front steps of the Burgess house. Millie's sheet-draped body lay in the yard a few feet away.

"What do you have for us, Chief?" asked Hunter as he sat down next to Valmonde.

"A couple of murder suicides within a few hours of each other," Valmonde said. "The circumstances of each are so similar that I don't think it was a coincidence."

He proceeded to explain both events. Hunter, Lorena and DuCassal listened quietly until he'd finished.

"This may or may not be coincidental," Hunter said. "You say both woman apparently decided to murder their families for no reason?"

"As far as I know," Valmonde said. "None of the neighbors reported anythin' unusual or remembered hearing any arguments. Everybody we talked to said that both families were pretty happy and got along well with each other.

I can see how one person might suddenly go off and murder somebody then feel guilty about it and decide to kill herself. But two in less than a week? That's strange even for New Orleans!"

"Let's have a look inside," Hunter said.

Valmonde escorted them into the kitchen where Calvin's bloody corpse still lay sprawled on the floor. Hunter knelt beside him and rolled him over.

"The first strike was to his back. He never saw it coming. The other wounds were inflicted after he was down," he said. "How long were they married?"

"Six years," Valmonde said.

"Any children?" asked Lorena.

"None," Valmonde replied.

They went upstairs to examine the balcony. Finding nothing out of the ordinary, they walked out of the house. Hunter looked up at the balcony and shook his head.

"You said the first one was exactly like this?" he asked.

"So damned close it's scary," Valmonde said. "What do you think?"

"I don't know what to think, Chief," Hunter admitted. "The only thing we can do now is see if anyone else ends up like this. If not, then this was all just a sad coincidence. If it happens again, we may be dealing with something supernatural."

"Makes sense," Valmonde agreed. "Let's hope this is the end of this."

Hunter nodded.

Savannah.

Things had been quiet in the city for the past week, thanks to a stubborn storm front that drenched the area with heavy rains each night.

Carmello and Riccardo spent most of each day with the O'Hara girls, touring, going to fine restaurants and attending several parties at some of Savannah's grander homes. It seemed that everyone in the city wanted to have them as party guests. Naturally, the girls went everywhere with them.

In fact, the four were just about inseparable now—much to the delight of Maureen. In fact, she was already getting prices from local caterers in preparation for the double wedding she was sure would come.

At night, the Slayers walked through the squares and streets of the city.

And all remained peaceful—and would remain so until the storm system moved back out to sea.

New Orleans.

Three more days passed.

Valmonde had almost relaxed his guard. He was about to write the murder-suicides off as a bizarre coincidence and close the book on the case.

Then lightning struck a third time.

Charlotte Webber, a pretty, 15 year old girl with an unassuming personality, cheerfully cut her father's throat while he slept on the sofa. The sound of his body hitting the floor as he rolled off the sofa, brought her mother into the living room on the run.

As soon as she entered the room, Charlotte drove the knife into her chest again and again. When she was certain that both of her parents were dead, Charlotte dropped the murder weapon and walked upstairs to the master bedroom.

Five minutes later, horrified neighbors and tourists watched as Charlotte threw herself from the gallery and onto Bourbon Street.

Valmonde, Hunter, Lorena and DuCassal arrived on the scene an hour later. Three of Valmonde's men had already sealed off the house and another was standing guard over Charlotte's broken body.

"That's three murder-suicides in less than a week," Valmonde said. "In all three cases, a woman, either a daughter or a wife, murdered everyone in the family then jumped off a balcony. This is too crazy to be a coincidence."

"I agree. Someone or something is behind this. Something very malevolent and vengeful," Hunter said.

"You mean like a pissed off ghost or somethin'?" Valmonde asked.

"A *very pissed off* ghost," Hunter said. "Since all of the murders are alike, they all have to be connected in some way. Someone targeted these families for a reason. We just need to find out what that reason is."

"I think I might have somethin' for you along those lines," Valmonde said. "I'll have to check the files to be sure."

"You *knew* these people?" Hunter asked.

"In a way," Valmonde replied. "But I want to make sure before I open my big mouth and put my foot in it. I'll get back to you later."

Hunter nodded.

"In the meantime, we'll go consult with Minerva. Maybe she can help make sense of this," he said.

Minerva listened as Hunter told her about the odd series of murder-suicides. She sipped her herbal tea, put the cup down on the saucer and nodded.

"From the description of the crimes, I think you might be dealing with something the Manila Men called an aswang," she said.

"What's that?" asked Hunter.

"Aswang was their word for many types of supernatural creatures. They could be vampires. Or werewolves. Or shapeshifters or even vengeful spirits," Minerva said.

"This seems to fit into the vengeful spirit category," Hunter said.

"I agree. Now you need to find out who that spirit is and why she is targeting those particular families," Minerva said.

"She?" asked Lorena.

"Yes. When it's vengeful spirit, the aswang is always female. Somewhere out there is a very angry spirit of a woman who has been deeply wronged or hurt. Enough so that she has returned from across the river to get revenge on those who wronged her," Minerva said.

"That means there's a connection between her victims," Hunter said.

"Without a doubt," DuCassal agreed.

"An aswang can't physically harm anyone herself. She needs a live human being to work through. She enters their bodies, takes control, and uses them to kill her targets," Minerva said.

"But why does she force them to commit suicide afterward?" asked Hunter.

"Once the deed is done, she must leave the body in order to finish her mission. She can only do this *after* the host is dead. So she forces the host to kill herself," Minerva explained.

"That's rough on the host," DuCassal said.

"Very," Hunter agreed. "How do we get rid of this thing?"

"According to the old legends, you kill it the same way you would kill a vampire. You drive a stake through its heart, behead it and burn it," Minerva replied.

"But that would also kill the host," Lorena pointed out.

"There h*as* to be another way," Hunter said.

"You could try to trap it. Wait for it to enter the host, then tie the host up and bring her to the temple. I may be able to exorcise the aswang. I'm not sure because I've never had to deal with one before. I'll have to do more research on this," Minerva suggested.

"To do that, we'll have to know in advance who her next intended victim is," Hunter said. "Valmonde said he thought there might be some connection."

"Let's go back to the station. Perhaps he has come up with something by now," DuCassal said.

Valmonde was seated behind his desk eating lunch when they walked in. He looked up and nodded as they sat down.

"I knew there was a connection," he said. "I just wanted to make sure I got the facts straight before I said anythin'."

"What do you have?" asked Hunter.

"About 16 years ago, four young hoodlums broke into a house on Tchoupitoulas originally to rob the place. They came across Sally Marquette and her young daughter, Helen, in an upstairs bedroom and decided to have a little fun. They took turns raping both of them. In between, they burned them with cigars, slashed them with knives and generally beat them until they were unrecognizable.

They were careless—or drunk—or both. They didn't try to shut either of the girls up.

Neighbors heard the screams and called us in.

I was the arresting officer at the time. Sam was there, too. We dragged them bastards into the station and a judge refused to set bail. The ladies ended up in the hospital where Sally died a day later from the 'hysterectomy' Calvin Burgess gave her. Helen died two weeks later. She never did come out of her coma," Valmonde said.

"These fellas were some of the wildest bastards in the whole city. They were in and out of trouble all of the time. Each time, their daddies came and bailed them out. Most of it was minor stuff.," he added.

"What happened? Did they go to trial?" asked Lorena.

"You might call it a trial," Valmonde said.

"I seem to remember that one. It was quite a sensation," DuCassal said.

"The trial was one of the great travesties of justice in New Orleans history," Valmonde said. "I caught those fellers red handed. They were as guilty as all Hell but that sorry excuse for a jury found them innocent of all charges. Their daddies paid the jurors off and they walked. I was never so disgusted in my life as I was that day."

He got up and poured himself another cup of coffee then walked to the window and looked out as he sipped.

"A bunch of us took up a collection to pay for the funeral. We laid Helen and her mother to rest in a small, unmarked vault over in Lafayette Number Two. It was the lease we could do for them," he said.

He sat back down and looked at Hunter.

"Funny thing. About a month afterward, the foreman of that so-called jury got himself shot for cheatin' at cards. Within six months, half the members of that jury ended up dead due to accidents or heart attacks. They've been steadily dyin' ever since. I don't think any of them are left now," he said.

"Looks as if someone's been going after them for years," Hunter said.

"Sure does. But their deaths seemed almost natural when compared with the killin's," Valmonde said. "What did Minerva say it was?"

"She said it was something called an aswang," Hunter replied.

"Your aswang wants them to know she's after them," Valmonde said.

"These are certainly acts of revenge carried to the extreme," DuCassal said.

Hunter explained what Minerva told them about the aswang. Valmonde nodded.

"If it's one of the ladies behind this, she's Hell bent on seein' that justice is served," he said. "I'd almost like to see her get her way, too."

"Who's left of that little band of murderers?" asked Hunter.

"That would be Pericles Jones," Valmonde said. "He lives over on Terpsichore with his wife Eppie and two kids."

"Any of them girls?" asked Hunter.

"Nope. They've got two sons," Valmonde replied.

"That means the aswang will try to use Eppie. So far, all of the murderers have been women. Apparently, the aswang prefers to use them for some reason," Hunter said.

"Maybe it's because women have weaker wills than most men?" DuCassal suggested.

Hunter shrugged.

"Let's go over there," he said.

"Are you going to try and save Jones?" asked Valmonde as he grabbed his hat.

"I don't give a rat's ass what happens to *him*. It's his *family* I'm concerned with," Hunter replied.

A half hour later, they were in the living room of a modest brick home on Terpsichore with Pericles Jones, his pretty wife Eppie and their two young sons. Hunter explained what was happening. The more he explained it, the more Pericles seemed to sink into the cushions of the old sofa.

"Did you really do such horrible things, Per?" Eppie asked.

"Yes, I did. And I've been having nightmares about it ever since. There's not a day that goes by that I don't beg God for forgiveness, even though I know I'm going to Hell for what I did. I never imagined it would one day fall on you and the boys," Pericles said.

"If it were up to me, I'd let that thing kill you," Hunter said. "But there's more to this that just saving your worthless ass."

"I don't care what happens to me, Hunter. I want you to save Eppie and my boys. I don't want that thing to harm them," Pericles said softly.

"That's why we've come," Hunter assured him.

"I really appreciate that. But how are you going to go about it?" Pericles asked.

"The most important thing is to try and keep the aswang from taking control of Eppie," Hunter explained. "If we stop her before she can enter Eppie's body, we may be able to either drive her away or kill her."

"What if you can't stop it?" asked Pericles. "What then?"

"We'll have to tie Eppie up to keep her from killing you and the boys. Then, with any luck, Minerva will be able to exorcise the aswang from her and trap it somehow," Hunter said.

Eppie stared at him.

"What if she can't, Mr. Hunter?" she asked.

"We'll cross that bridge when we come to it. I'll do everything in my power to keep you from being harmed in any way," he promised.

They stayed the night to see what would happen.

Several hours passed.

Hunter nodded off in the parlor. DuCassal, who stayed in the master bedroom with Pericles, did the same. Only Lorena stayed awake and she was in the kitchen speaking with Eppie when she noticed a strange wisp of smoke enter through the open window. The smoke went straight for Eppie, swirled around her a few seconds, and then entered her body through her eyes.

Lorena watched as Eppie lowered her head for a moment. When she looked up, the calm, friendly Eppie had changed into a twisted, dark version of herself. Eppie smiled at Lorena then walked to the counter. She took a knife from the drawer and darted from the kitchen.

Lorena followed her to the hallway and watched as she raced upstairs. Rather than follow her, Lorena went into the living room to get Hunter.

Eppie entered the bedroom holding the large butcher knife in her right hand. She walked over to the bed where Pericles lay sleeping, grinned evilly and raised the knife above her head. Before she could deliver the fatal blow, DuCassal sped across the room and seized her wrist.

Eppie spun around and backhanded him.

The blow, which was unexpectedly powerful, sent DuCassal flying across the room where he crashed into the mirrored armoire.

The commotion woke Pericles who rolled out of bed just in time to avoid the knife which Eppie planted in the middle of his pillow. She turned and went after him—only to be sent to the floor by a hard right cross from Hunter who had just entered the room with Lorena.

Before she could recover, Hunter and Lorena dragged her to the bed and bound her to the frame by her wrists and ankles. When she attempted to break her bonds, the sight of Hunter's revolver pointed directly at her face quieted her.

"That's a good girl," Hunter said. "Stay quiet and maybe you'll live."

Pericles walked over and looked into his wife's hostile eyes.

"She nearly got me," he said. "Is that really Eppie or that aswang thing?"

"Both," Hunter said. "We managed to trap it. Now comes the hard part."

"You mean getting that thing out of her?" Pericles asked.

Hunter nodded.

"We'll take her to Minerva. She'll have to take it from here," he said.

"What do you want me to do?" asked Pericles.

"Stay here and wait for us to come back. With any luck, we'll bring Eppie with us—alive," Hunter replied as he and DuCassal untied Eppie from the bed and dragged her from the house.

Twenty minutes later, they walked into the temple and forced Eppie to sit in a high backed chair.

"Is it in her?" Minerva asked.

"It sure as Hell is," DuCassal replied. "Be careful, It's very strong."

Minerva sat down in front of Eppie and looked into her eyes. After a while, she shook her head.

"The spirit inside of her is filled with deep hatred. It can't rest until it finishes what it came to do," she said.

"Kill Pericles Jones," Lorena said.

"Exactly," Minerva said.

"Pericles deserves to die for his crime," Hunter said. "But Eppie—and those other women—didn't. We have to get that thing out of her."

"The only way to kill it is to kill the host," Minerva said as she examined Eppie.

"That would be very rough on Mrs. Jones," Lorena pointed out.

"Very," Hunter agreed. "Is there another way around this?"

"I've got something in mind, but I'll need another host to drive the aswang into. I'll need the corpse of a young, recently deceased woman," Minerva said.

"How recent?" asked Hunter.

"No more than 72 hours," Minerva replied.

"We could check the morgue. Maybe we'll get lucky," DuCassal suggested.

"In the meantime, I'll keep Eppie tied up down here so she can't hurt anyone. As long as she stays alive, the aswang can't leave her body," Minerva said.

The night surgeon stared at them.

"You need what?" he asked as if he wasn't sure what they'd asked.

"A cadaver. Someone young and female and she has to have died within the last two days," Hunter repeated.

"Do you have anyone like that right now? It's very urgent!" Lorena emphasized.

"As a matter of fact, we do. She's downstairs in the morgue right now. They found her last night. So far, no one has claimed her," the surgeon said as he took the heavy key from the hook on the wall.

They followed him downstairs and into the morgue.

Once inside, the surgeon walked over to a wall containing 12 coolers and pulled open the drawer on the lower left side. Then he pulled back the white sheet to reveal a rather serene looking young woman with light brown hair.

"No one knows who she is," the surgeon said. "I guess she's about 25 or so. She died of an apparent drug overdose. The wagon brought her in late last night. She had no money or I.D. on her."

"She's perfect," Hunter said. "We need to borrow her for a few hours."

"Seeing as it's you, Hunter, I guess it's alright. Just bring her back when you're through—if you can," the surgeon said.

Lorena walked over and touched the girl's forehead. She shook her head, then checked the sides of her neck.

"Just as I thought," she said as she pointed to the two small punctures on the woman's neck. "She didn't die of an overdose. A vampire killed her."

The surgeon looked startled.

"I don't know how the morgue boys missed that. It's not mentioned in their report," he said. "I wonder why?"

"I suggest that you keep an eye on your crew," Hunter said. "If you notice anything unusual about them, let me know. Right now, we have something more important to take care of."

He lifted the body and slung it over his shoulder. Lorena grabbed the sheet and covered her as best as she could. The surgeon escorted them back to the main lobby and wished them luck.

"That was close," he said as he shut the door after them. "Next time, I won't be so careless."

"That surgeon is a vampire," Lorena said as they loaded the cadaver into the luggage compartment of DuCassal's carriage.

"I know. Do you think he's the one who killed her?" Hunter said as he helped her aboard.

"No. I think she was already dead when they brought her there. He just drained her of some blood to satisfy his needs," Lorena said.

"Then there's no need to go after him as long as he only takes blood from recently dead people or willing sources," Hunter said. "If he goes after anyone who doesn't want to donate to his blood bank, we'll step in."

DuCassal leaned out the window and shouted up to the driver.

"Take us to Minerva's, George!"

Minerva was dressed in her ceremonial robes when they arrived. She smiled when she saw the cadaver draped over Hunter's shoulder.

"She'll do," Minerva said after she examined the body.

As Minerva instructed, they took both Eppie and the cadaver out into the courtyard and staked them hands and feet to the ground.

Minerva took out a bag of sea salt and drew a large circle on the ground around both Eppie and the cadaver.

"This will keep the aswang from getting too far when I force her from Eppie," she explained. "Sea salt is pure and it comes from the ocean. Evil spirits can't cross over a line that's made from it."

She took out a small parchment tied with a red ribbon. Then she looked back at them.

"You need to stand back about 20 feet or so. I don't want anyone's energy messing with the spell," she instructed.

They did as she asked and watched as she placed three different colored candles on the floor between the cadaver and Eppie and lit them. Then she knelt in front of Eppie and read the spell.

Eppie cried, screamed, cursed and spasmed as the spell slowly took effect. Minerva repeated it three times. Each time, she snuffed out one of the candles with her fingertips. Soon, a light mist emerged from Eppie's body, hovered over Minerva, and then slowly entered the cadaver.

When she was certain that the aswang had been transferred to the cadaver, Minerva drove the bamboo spear through its heart and into the ground beneath it. The cadaver twitched and jumped around a few times, then became still.

"Is it dead?" asked Hunter.

"No. But it ain't going anywhere. I staked it to the ground," Minerva said.

"Now what?" asked Hunter.

"You deal with it like you would any vampire. You behead it and burn the body," Minerva replied as she stepped back.

Hunter drew his katana and severed the head with one deft stroke. He sheathed the weapon, then doused both the head and torso with blessed oil and ignited it. As the smoke and flames consumed the body, the air around them echoed with a horrific scream that was enough to shatter a few nearby window panes. The scream lasted only a few seconds, then everything fell silent.

"That was the sound of an aswang dying," Minerva said. "It's over."

Eppie looked at them and smiled weakly.

"Thank you all from the bottom of my heart," she said. "You saved me and my family from what would have been a terrible death."

They took Eppie home in DuCassal's carriage then rode over to the station to tell Valmonde what happened.

"What should I do about Pericles? He did admit he had a hand in killin' those two women," Valmonde asked.

"That's up to you, Chief," Hunter said. "Personally, I'd leave him be. He'll be living in his own private Hell for the rest of his life. Angola won't be of any use at this point. Besides, Eppie and his sons need him more than Angola needs another prisoner. There's no sense punishing them for his crimes."

"I guess you're right, Hunter. Eppie and the boys would suffer most and they had nothin' to do with any of this," Valmonde agreed.

"That's very generous of you, mon cher," Lorena said.

"Charles has always had a soft spot for children," DuCassal said.

Hunter smiled.

"If Pericles Jones was a single man, I would have allowed the aswang to exact her revenge. In this case, I decided to allow reason to prevail over my sense of justice," he explained.

"Besides, more than enough innocent people have been killed to satisfy that witch's lust for vengeance. Even had she managed to kill Jones, she might not have stopped. We just couldn't take that chance," he added.

"So for the good of the city, Jones gets to walk again," Valmonde said.

"Not really, Chief. His secret's out in the open. Now he has to live with it," Hunter said.

"That's somethin' I sure would hate to live with. It'll be especially hard now that his family knows what he did," Valmonde agreed. "Eppie and the boys will never feel the same about him again."

"And that will be a punishment worse than death," Hunter said.

They left the station and climbed into DuCassal's waiting carriage.

"Where to?" he asked.

"How about the Court of Two Sisters?" Lorena suggested. "It's almost time for brunch."

"The Court it is!" DuCassal agreed.

Four a.m.

A hooded female figure walked down an alley and listened at the heavy wooden door. Satisfied that the one she sought was within, she stepped back and kicked the door open. The loud bang startled the group of men who were inside watching as another man in a black mask raped a screaming little girl from behind for the amusement of the crowd. The man stopped when the intruder approached the stage and drew her katana.

"Who in Hell are you to come bargin' in here? This is a private club!" a man close to stage said as he motioned for four larger, muscular men to grab her.

"I'm your worst night mare—and this club is *closed!*" the woman said as she easily avoided the four goons and deftly lopped off various parts of their anatomies with her blade. Within moments, all four lay dying on the floor near the stage as pools of blood spread from beneath them.

"Anyone else who doesn't wish to die, had better leave now!" the woman said.

The rest of the men fled for their lives without uttering a sound.

The woman stepped up to the manager and grabbed him by the throat. She could feel him trembling now. His heart was racing out of control and he was sweating profusely. She laughed then looked at the man on the stage, who still had his member inside the girl.

"Don't you dare move," she instructed. "Stay right where you are if you know what's good for you."

The man on the stage pulled out of the girl and stared in horror as the woman bared her fangs and sunk them into the manager's throat. Less than a minute later, his pale, lifeless corpse thudded to the floor.

The man on the stage screamed and tried to run for the back door only to be grabbed from behind and slammed face-first to the floor. The woman turned him over and gripped his throat.

"I was only going to bring you into the station. But you tried to run. I told you not to do that…" she said as she sunk her fangs into his neck.

An hour later, Hannah Morii dropped the terrified little girl—and the two small boys she found chained to a post in a back room—off at the Basin Street station. Valmonde smiled and thanked her for her service to the city as he handed her the envelope containing the bounty money.

Hannah stuffed it into her pocket and left.

"I'm startin' to think she's more ruthless than Lorena," Valmonde said to Sam. "She doesn't even pretend to take prisoners!"

"Well, it ain't like she's killing anybody that don't need it," Sam said.

Hannah laughed as she walked back to her shop. She felt strong and energetic. More so than ever before. She was feeding herself and doing the city a great service at the same time. The two tonight made nine she'd done in since Lorena turned her.

Nine in less than two months.

It was so easy to hunt humans.

Even easier to kill them.

And their numbers were limitless.

And their blood tasted so good!

"I should have done this years ago!" she said as she entered her shop and removed her cloak.

CHAPTER EIGHT:
The Wild Hunt

Eight p.m.

Another steamy night in Savannah.

Carmello and Riccardo were making their usual patrol of the Hostess City. They walked along Broughton and turned south on Drayton. They strolled past stately mansions, dimly lit restaurants and bars and small, neat homes. Each street was lines with beautiful, ancient live oaks whose moss-covered branches cast eerie shadows in the soft glare of the street lamps.

And the streets were strangely deserted, save for a young woman with a shopping basket on the crook of her left arm who passed them as they crossed York Street. She smiled at them, said "evening" and hurried past. They tipped their hats and smiled back.

As soon as they hit the next sidewalk, the lights became obscured by a strange thick fog that suddenly rolled in from everywhere. They stopped and watched as the fog obscured buildings, trees and street lamps. It was so dense, everything within sight had been reduced to fuzzy shadows.

That's when they heard it.

A clear, sharp note from a distant horn. It, like the fog, came from everywhere.

Almost instantly, Savannah was gone. The brothers now found themselves standing in the middle of a fog-shrouded wasteland of leafless trees, prickly brush and sharp rocks. The horn sounded again.

This time, it was closer.

The horn was followed by loud howls and barks.

A moment later, the young woman with the shopping basket came running toward them. She stopped and clutched Riccardo's arm as she peered nervously into the fog.

"What's happening?" she asked. "What happened to the city?"

Riccardo was about to try and say something to comfort her when the first of the wolves emerged from the fog. It glared at them with its fiery red eyes, then emitted a series of howls, which were quickly answered by a canine chorus.

The woman cowered behind the brothers as eight more massive wolves appeared and began to circle them. Each of them moved slowly as they kept their evil gaze on the three people standing between them.

"Those are the second biggest wolves I've ever seen!" Carmello said.

Riccardo shot him a look that said he was not amused and drew his revolver. Carmello did the same, although he wondered what use bullets would be against such creatures.

A few moments later, an imposing figure astride a coal-black horse rode slowly up to them and stared at the woman. Then he raised his right hand and pointed at her.

The wolves snarled and moved in.

Carmello responded by firing shots at the nearest one. To his dismay, the bullets had no affect on the creature. In fact, the wolf ignored him completely and kept its eyes on the terrified woman.

Then it leaped.

Riccardo tried to shield her with his body but the animal passed right through him. The woman screamed, tossed away her heavy basket and began running for her life into the fog. The wolves gave chase—and so did the brothers.

But they became hopelessly lost in the ever thickening fog. They stopped to get their bearings.

That's when they heard her scream.

The scream was followed by growls, barks and howls as the wolves brought the terrified woman down and tore her to pieces while she cried for help.

The brothers ran in the direction of the sounds. When they reached her, the wolves stopped what they were doing and walked away as the horn once more resounded through the fog. They watched helplessly as they wolves vanished into the fog. A few minutes later, the fog also vanished.

They found themselves standing in the middle of Chippewa Square not thirty yards from the pitiful, bloody remains of the young woman.

The Wild Huntsman had claimed yet another victim.

"*Now* do you believe the legend?" Carmello asked.

"Oh, Hell yes!" Riccardo answered as he knocked the mud off his hat. "Now that we know he's real, how do we get rid of him? It's not like we can politely ask him to leave."

"That's a good question," Carmello agreed.

"I know. Do you have a good answer?" asked Riccardo as they walked back to Bay Street.

"We'll need some help. Someone who knows magic or voodoo. What we need is a *witch*," Carmello said.

"That makes sense. A city as old as Savannah must have several witches. Let's talk to O'Hara. Maybe he can steer us to one," Riccardo said.

New Orleans, 11p.m.

Marcie Hall, a pretty, young woman with an infectious smile, left her job at Morrow's Boutique on Magazine Street. As she walked along Delachaise toward St. Charles to catch the streetcar home, she failed to notice the tall, lean figure watching her from a shadowy doorway.

The man waited until she crossed the street then followed.

When she stopped, he stopped.

When she crossed Chestnut Street, he crossed.

He kept himself at a distance so she wouldn't notice he was stalking her.

She was so young.

So naïve.

And she'd be an easy kill.

Marcie crossed Colisuem.

The man waited a few seconds, then crossed behind her, making sure that he kept her in sight. When the time was right, and the streets were deserted, he'd transform himself into a rougarou and pounce on his prey.

It would be quick.

Too quick for anyone to save her.

Marcie reached the stop at St. Charles and waited. The streetcar would arrive in ten minutes and no one else was around.

Her stalker smiled and moved silently toward her from behind. Just as he was about to make his move, he was distracted by someone striking a match as he leaned against a tree not ten feet from him. He watched as the strange man in an even stranger-looking mask that concealed only part of his face. Lit a cigar and puffed it. As he did, the rougarou wondered how he had missed seeing him, especially with all of his heightened senses.

"I wouldn't if I were you," the man said.

"Oh? And just who are *you* to tell me what I should or shouldn't do?" the rougarou asked.

"I am your worst nightmare," the man replied as he blew smoke in his direction. "Your very worst nightmare."

By now, Marci had heard their conversation. She turned around as the man in the mask took another puff of his cigar and smiled at her stalker. The smile obviously angered him to no end.

"We'll see about that!" the rougarou said as he transformed himself.

Marcie stared in shock as the man turned into a rougarou. She was transfixed to the spot. Too curious to look away and far too frightened to run.

The rougarou snarled and beat his chest. The man in the mask laughed at his theatrics as he put out the cigar and removed his hat and cape.

The rougarou leapt straight at him, intending to take this busybody down with one quick strike. Instead, the man seized him by the throat and brutally slammed him to the pavement.

The stunned creature watched helplessly as his foe almost instantly transformed into a larger, darker version of a rougarou and sank his teeth into his throat.

It was at that last instant of his life that he realized who his opponent was.

"Alejandro!" he said with his dying breath.

Marcie, of course, fainted.

When she regained consciousness, she was on the streetcar and heading for home…

New Orleans, three a.m.

Lorena watched as Hunter tossed and turned next to her. She knew he was falling into another deep, dark sleep.

One that was normally haunted by terrifying visions of his past.

She looked at him and wondered where this nightmare was taking him.

This time, it was different.

He saw a man dressed in 15th century garb seated in a study that was dimly illuminated by two large candles on his desk. The man was writing on a parchment with a large quill. He saw the man from behind and had the strangest sensation that he was in the room with him. And that he should know who he is.

He watched as a second man approached the one at the desk slowly. Silently.

The man at the desk turned for some reason and saw his stalker.

"You!" he cried as he stood up.

"Of course it's me. You didn't think that you could be rid of me *that* easily, did you, my old friend?" the other man said.

"But you're *dead!*" the first man said.

"I assure you that I am quite alive," the second replied smugly. "I will *always* live, despite your many attempts to render me otherwise."

"What do you want here? Be gone lest I summon the guards!" the first man threatened.

The second man laughed.

It was a laugh filled with evil intent.

"Your guards cannot save you now. No one can," he said as he stepped toward him. 'I told you that you couldn't kill me so easily. I warned you that I would return—and I have. You've betrayed me for the last time, Geogi."

"You don't mean to kill me, do you?" the first man said as he backed away in terror.

"No—I'm going to do something far worse than that!" the second man replied as he seized him by the throat....

Hunter woke with a start.

As usual, he was covered with sweat.

He looked around and smiled when he saw Lorena.

"What was it? The battles again?" she asked as she touched his shoulder.

"No. Something different. Something I've never dreamt before," Hunter replied as he got up and dressed.

She watched until he was finished. When he left the room, she dressed. She waited until she heard the front door open and shut, then went out after him. Hunter's dreams were becoming more frequent.

More vivid.

They used to disrupt his sleep once or twice a month. Now, he was having them every week.

Sometimes, twice per week.

She wondered if this had anything to do with the Baron? Could he be the cause of the dreams?

She smiled.

"I wouldn't put anything past that monster!" she said as she followed Hunter toward the French Quarter.

Hunter walked along Burgundy and turned when he reached St. Ann. Before he'd gone a block, the all-too-familiar mists rose up around him and obscured everything in sight. He stopped and waited.

Seconds later, Madame Laveau appeared and smiled when she saw him.

"Good evening, Hunter," she greeted.

"Good evening, Marie. I'm glad to see that you're out and about tonight," he replied as he touched the brim of his hat.

"I saw your dream. I see *all* your dreams," Madame Laveau said smugly.

"This one was different," he said.

"I know," she said.

"The man in the dream. The one I couldn't see. Was that me?" he asked.

"What do *you* think?" she countered. "Do you believe it was you?"

"I don't know what to believe," he replied.

"Do you w*ant* him to be you?" she teased.

"No. There was something very foul about him. Something dark and evil," Hunter replied. "I don't want to believe that I was ever like him or that I could ever be like him. Is it me?"

She laughed.

Her laugh irritated him. He fought off the urge to scream.

"You aren't anything at all like the man in your dream," she assured him. "Does that make you feel better?"

"Yes—no! Hell, I don't know!" Hunter said in frustration.

"You know the answer, Hunter. You just don't want to let yourself believe it. Perhaps that is one door that is best left locked," Madame Laveau said.

Before Hunter to say anything else, both Marie Laveau and the mist were gone. He uttered his usual string of epithets and headed for Bourbon Street.

Lorena caught up with him and hooked arms.

He smiled.

"Let's go to the Dragon," she suggested.

St. Louis Cathedral, four a.m.

Father Paul walked out of the back office and stopped when he saw the hooded figure seated in the front row of pews. The figure had his head down as if her were praying. Paul walked over and tapped the rail in front of him to get his attention. The man looked up and bared his fangs.

Paul stepped back.

"What are *you* doing here?" he demanded.

"I'm thirsty. I thought I'd drop in for a drink," the vampire replied smoothly as he stood and removed his cloak.

"There are several bars on Decatur," Paul suggested. "You can try one of them."

"They don't serve what I want," the vampire said as he stepped out of the pew and walked toward him.

Paul decided to go for a beaker of holy water on the altar. But the vampire attacked first. He seized Paul by the throat and threw him against the rail of the altar. Before Paul could get up, the vampire pounced on him from behind and grabbed his head. Paul resisted with all of his strength as the creature tried to twist his head in order to get at his neck.

When the vampire bared his fangs to deliver what would be a fatal bite, Paul pulled the Bowie knife from his boot and drove it up into the soft underside of the creature's chin until the point burst through the top of his skull. He then slammed the hilt as hard as he could with the palm of his hand to drive the weapon even deeper.

The startled vampire fell backwards and hit the floor, gurgling blood all the way.

Paul acted quickly.

He took a brass candlestick from the altar and plunged it into the vampire's chest with all of his might. Then he twisted it until the creature's heart popped.

He then used the Bowie knife to decapitate the vampire. This done, he dragged the head and torso out into the back garden and set them on fire.

"Stupid bastard!" he sneered as he watched the flames consume the body.

He returned to the church to wipe the blood off the floor but stopped in his tracks when he saw the tall, dark-haired man dressed in black standing in the middle of the aisle. Paul sneered and strode over to him.

"One of yours?" he asked as he nodded at the blood stain.

"I have underestimated you. You fight very well for a priest," the vampire said.

"I wasn't *always* a priest," Paul said. "May I assume that I am speaking to the Baron?"

"At your service," the Baron assured him with a slight bow of his head.

He looked down at the blood.

"He was supposed to kill you and leave a note on your body," the Baron said. "I guess I will have to do this myself."

"Why would he serve the likes of you?" asked Paul.

"He had no choice. I *made* him," the Baron replied.

"You didn't do a very good job of it," Paul sneered.

"One can only work with the materials that are available," the Baron said.

"If you're here for a fight, bring it. If not, state your business and get out of my church," Paul said with more than a little irritation.

"Very well. I want you to deliver a message to Hunter and Lorena. Tell them to meet me at midnight tomorrow in the chapel of St. Mary," the Baron said. "Tell them I think it is time we had a little talk."

"That's all?" Paul asked.

"That is all," the Baron said as he walked toward the front door. "I bid you good evening, Father."

Paul watched as he left the church. He looked down at the pool of blood and shook his head.

"First things first," he said as he went to the storage closet to get a mop and bucket.

It was a cool, clear night in Savannah.

Following O'Hara's advice, Carmello and Riccardo left their hotel and walked along River Street until they spotted the old black and white sign.

They stopped and read.

The white lettering proclaimed that the woman upstairs read palms and made love potions. It also had an arrow pointing upward.

"This has to be it," Carmello said.

"Let's give it a try," Riccardo agreed.

They walked up the narrow stairway and found themselves standing in a large, open loft filled with all sorts of magic and voodoo paraphernalia.

A small, white-haired woman in a blue frock was seated in a high backed rocking chair knitting something. She smiled when they approached.

"Are you Miss Anna?" asked Carmello.

"I am," she replied without looking up.

"We're--," Carmello began.

"I *know* who you are. I also know why you're here," Miss Anna said. "You want to know who summoned the Huntsman. I can find out, but it will cost you."

"How much?" asked Riccardo.

"I don't mean money," she said with a grin.

"Neither do *I*," Riccardo assured her.

She laughed.

"Okay then. You must bring me the eyes—intact—of one of his wolves. Then I'll need something personal from you and one of his victims," she instructed. "It has to be something that is always with you. Understand?"

"That means we'll have to kill one of his wolves," Carmello said.

"That's right," Anna nodded.

"Just how on Earth can we do *that*?" asked Riccardo.

"Silver bullets—but you'll have to be sure and shoot it through the heart or the bullet will only pass through," Anna explained.

"Why don't we just shoot the Huntsman?" asked Carmello.

Anna laughed.

"Nothing on God's Earth can harm the Huntsman. When you bring down the wolf, the rest of the pack should lose interest in the hunt and retreat," she said.

"What of they don't?" asked Riccardo.

"In that case, they'll tear you limb from limb!" Anna said.

They left and headed back to the hotel.

"It's a good thing we Slayers always carry a box of silver bullets with us when we travel," Carmello said as he tossed his hat on a nearby chair inside the room. "But pistols won't do. They aren't accurate enough. We'll have time to make only one shot and it has to hit its mark."

"We can use the sniper rifle," Riccardo said as he went to the closet and took out a long, thin box.

He placed it on the bed and opened it.

Carmello watched as he assembled the weapon, then held it up to examine the scope. He then tossed it to Carmello, who raised it and looked through the scope.

"Infra red?" he asked.

Carmello smiled.

"Brother Parker made it. He followed an ancient blueprint from the late wars of the First Age. All you need do is get your target in the crosshairs and fire. It has an effective range of 2,500 yards," Riccardo explained.

"Ever fire it?" Carmello asked.

"Only for target practice. It has a pretty good kick," Riccardo said.

"Then you'll have to bring the wolf down," Carmello said as he passed the rifle to him. "You're more familiar with this weapon than I am and I have no time for practice."

Riccardo nodded.

"I'll do my best," he said. "We're properly armed. All we need now is some fog."

"WWHD," Carmello said.

"What does that mean?" asked Riccardo.

"What would Hunter do?" Carmello replied.

CHAPTER NINE:
The Meeting

St. Mary's was part of the ancient Ursuline Convent complex. The only way to reach the chapel was by going through the convent and entering a side door. After Hunter and Lorena rid the convent of the vampires who masqueraded as nuns, DuCassal used his considerable wealth and influence to turn the complex into a museum.

At five minutes to midnight, Hunter, Lorena and DuCassal walked up to the main gate of the convent. DuCassal pulled a key from his pocket and unlocked it.

"Do you want me to accompany you?" he asked.

"No. The Baron requested that only Lorena and I meet him. Wait here and be alert. If you here gunshots, come in and join the party," Hunter said.

"Bon chance, mes amis," DuCassal bade them as they walked through the gate.

He watched them walk across the garden and enter the convent.

"I would like to be a fly on the wall for this meeting. I think that will be a most interesting conversation," he said to himself as he sat down on a nearby bench.

Hunter and Lorena entered the chapel through the side door. They were surprised to find that the lights had been turned on. They looked around then walked to the front of the altar.

Hunter checked his watch.

"It's midnight," he said. "Where's the Baron?"

That's when they heard the unmistakable sounds of leather soled boots on the marble floor echoing through the chapel. They watched as the Baron approached and stopped less than 20 feet from them.

He bowed his head and smiled.

"Good evening. I am glad that you have decided to accept my invitation," he said.

"Let's cut to the chase, Baron. What do you want, vermin?" Hunter demanded.

The Baron scowled.

"Be careful whom you call vermin lest you discover that you defame yourself," he said.

"And what does that mean?" Hunter asked, his patience wearing thin.

The Baron stared into his eyes.

Almost immediately, images of fierce battles between mounted knights, chainmailed warriors and countless Turks flooded into his mind. In the background, he saw a flaming village and a dark, brooding castle high atop a hill. The battle faded and was quickly replaced by a man seated at a linen-covered table, eating dinner and laughing as soldiers impaled screaming Turks on wooden poles.

Then the flaming numerals 1462 appeared.

"Who *are* you?" the Baron asked.

Hunter stepped back and shook his head to drive the images out. The Baron took a step closer.

"Who are you?" he asked again.

More images flooded into Hunter's brain. He saw men in mail affixing jeweled turbans to the heads of screaming emissaries with iron spikes as the lord of the manor watched implacably from a high backed chair. When the screams became whimpers, he ordered his men to drag them out and tie them to their horses.

Again Hunter stepped back and shook the images from his head.

The Baron smiled.

"The answer to my question—and *ours*—lies hidden within your nightmares. Each image is but a tiny glimpse into the distant past and adds another small piece to the puzzle that has been plaguing you all these centuries. All you need do is unlock the door," he said.

"There are some doors that are best left shut," Hunter said. "After all this time, what does it matter?"

The Baron laughed.

"So you prefer to live out the rest of your long life in complete ignorance?" he taunted. "Are you *afraid* of what lies beyond that door? Are you afraid to learn the *truth*?"

"Who's truth? Yours or mine?" Hunter asked.

"Both, if you like," the Baron offered. "You and I intricately entwined with each other. In many ways, we are nearly inseparable."

"Enough of your games, Baron," Hunter snapped. "Why did you come to New Orleans?"

"I came to see *you*," the Baron replied. "We have a score to settle between us. I am weary of being hounded by the two of you. So I have come here to make you an offer."

"What kind of offer?" asked Lorena.

"A truce," the Baron replied.

"A truce? What type of truce?" asked Hunter.

"A very simple one. If you leave me alone, I shall leave you alone," the Baron offered.

"Leave you alone to roam the Earth to feed on humankind forever? And to create even more like you?" Hunter said. "I think not!"

The Baron turned to Lorena.

"And what have you to say to my offer?" he asked.

"No deal!" she said. "I swore an oath to kill you and by all that is unholy, I will do just that!"

The Baron laughed.

"You have tried many times. And you have failed each and every time. You shall fail again," he said smugly. "You are no match for me. I think you should reconsider."

"No deal!" they both reiterated.

"Is that your final answer?" the Baron asked.

They both nodded.

He sighed.

"In that case, we shall have to settle this matter once and forever," he said. "Either you will die or I will. But settled it will be."

"Name the time and the place," Hunter said.

"Washington Square Park at midnight, one week from tonight," the Baron said.

"We'll be there," Hunter promised.

The Baron grinned.

"I know," he said as he turned and walked out of the chapel.

DuCassal was still seated on the bench when the Baron walked up to him and tapped him on the shoulder. He tilted his hat back and squinted up at him.

"Are you Jean-Paul DuCassal?" the Baron asked.

"You have me at a disadvantage, sir," DuCassal said. "To whom do I have the pleasure of speaking?"

"I am Baron Georgi Konstantino Vlastrada—at your service," the Baron said with a smart bow of his head.

DuCassal rose and looked him in the eyes. The Baron noticed that he didn't even blink. He smiled.

"Are you a Slayer also?" he asked.

"I am not a professional, but I do what I can to help," DuCassal said modestly. "Some would say that I have become quite proficient at it."

The Baron smiled.

"I just challenged your friends to a showdown one week from tonight. I expect that you will also be there," he said.

"You can count on it," DuCassal said.

"I know," the Baron said as he walked through the gate and turned left.

DuCassal watched as he disappeared around the corner. Then he heard Hunter and Lorena walk up.

"So that is the Baron," DuCassal said.

Hunter nodded.

"He doesn't look like such a much," DuCassal said.

"In his case, looks are *very* deceiving, Jean-Paul," Hunter assured him.

"Do we face him alone?" Lorena asked.

"Not if we want to end this. If we face him alone like we did in the past, it would end the same as it always has and this soap opera would continue. He knows about *you*, Jean-Paul. But I don't think he knows about Hannah or Alejandro," Hunter said.

"You plan to bring them in on this?" DuCassal asked.

"Yes. They'll be our aces in the hole. With any luck, our superior numbers will tip the scales in our favor," Hunter replied.

"Is this Baron so powerful that it will take all five of us to defeat him?" DuCassal asked.

"Yes to both questions," Hunter said. "For this battle, we'll need to pull out all the stops. We'll have to use everything we have and hope it's enough."

"He must be one tough son of a bitch!" DuCassal remarked.

"That he is," Hunter assured him. "That's why we'll need all the help we can get. Any idea where we can find Alejandro?"

"He sometimes goes to the Dragon. We can start there," DuCassal suggested.

"We already know where to find Hannah," Lorena added.

Later that night, they entered the Dragon and looked around. DuCassal spotted Alejandro seated near a back window and pointed.

"There he is!" he said.

They walked over. Alejandro stopped puffing his cigar and invited them to sit down. He then signaled to the waitress to bring three more drinks.

"I'm drinking hand grenades tonight. I hope you will join me for at least one round," he said.

"We'd be glad to," DuCassal said as he placed his hat on the window sill.

"We need your help, Alejandro," Hunter said.

"Just ask and it is yours," Alejandro assured him. "I am at your service."

Hunter explained what was going on. The waitress brought their drinks over and Hunter continued to talk while they drank.

"I think you could be our ace in the hole," Hunter said.

Alejandro smiled as he puffed his cigar.

"I'd be happy to join your little party. It sounds like fun," he said.

"Don't take the Baron lightly. He's one tough bastard," Hunter warned.

"He may be all you say he is, but I guarantee that he has never in his long life encountered anyone like *me*. From where *I* sit, it is the Baron who should be worried," Alejandro said smugly.

Hunter smiled and slapped him on the back.

"You might be right," he said. "Meet us there an hour early. Don't show yourself until you feel the time is right."

"With my flair for dramatic entrances, that should not be a problem," Alejandro assured him.

From there, they walked over to Hannah's shop. Lorena looked through the window and saw her walking up the steps. She was dressed in her hunting outfit.

"Let me handle this alone," she said.

Hunter nodded.

Lorena walked around to the side of the building and scaled the wall. When she reached the open window to Hannah's bedroom, she slipped inside. Hannah's back was to her.

"Nice of you to drop by, Lorena," she said.

Lorena laughed.

She knew that Hannah had heard her scale the wall. Her senses were becoming stronger by the day.

Lorena noticed the lines of blood on the corners of Hannah's mouth.

"Been out for a snack?" she asked.

"Let's just say that Valmonde has one less vicious criminal to contend with," Hannah replied as she wiped the blood off.

"Aren't you feeding a little too often?" Lorena asked.

"I feed when the urge strikes me," Hannah said. "I have no control over that."

Lorena nodded, but she wondered if Hannah had developed too strong a taste for human blood. She was definitely feeding more often than she should. Perhaps, Lorena hoped, it was just her body's way of adapting to her change? She put the thoughts from her mind.

That's when they heard the front door to the shop open and shut.

"That's Hunter," Hannah said. "DuCassal, too. I can smell them."

They went down to greet them.

Hunter noticed that Hannah's eyes seemed both darker and brighter at the same time. He also sensed the power surging through her entire frame. The change was taking hold big time.

He explained what was happening.

Hannah nodded.

"You can count me in," she agreed. "He's one vampire lord this world can do without. I'll be there."

Hunter held up five fingers.

"That's all of us. One more week and we can write the final chapter in this saga," he said. "There's still one thing that bothers me. The Baron wasn't born a vampire. Somebody else turned him. I've always wondered who that is and if he still walks the Earth."

"Whoever made him must be quite ancient. That happened centuries ago," Lorena said. "The Baron had been around over two thousand years when he turned me."

"That makes him at least as old as *we* are, Charles," DuCassal said. "He must have been born sometime during the 15th century of the First Age."

Again, the flaming numerals 1462 flashed through Hunter's mind.

"Maybe *that's* what those numbers mean. They could mean the year 1462. But what makes that year so significant?" he asked.

"Wasn't that the period when the Turks tried to invade Eastern Europe?" asked DuCassal. "I believe they tried to invade Romania."

"That would also explain all the images of Turkish soldiers I see in my dreams. But what on Earth does any of it have to do with *me*?" Hunter said.

"After all this time, what does it really matter, eh, Charles? None of that is of any importance now," DuCassal said. "As they say, it's all ancient history. In our case, that is in the *literal* sense."

"I guess you're right, Jean-Paul," Hunter said. "Right now, we have the Baron to contend with."

Five p.m.

Minerva was praying in her temple when she got the strangest sensation of being watched. She completed her prayer, then turned to see if anyone was there. To her surprised, an all-too-familiar woman in a long white dress and blue scarf smiled at her from the doorway.

"Madame Laveau!" Minerva almost gasped.

"Good evening, my child. I didn't mean to interrupt," Madam Laveau said softly.

"I am honored by your presence," Minerva said.

"This is not a social call. You *know* why I'm here," Madame Laveau said.

"Hunter's showdown with the Baron," Minerva stated.

Madam Laveau nodded.

"This will be the turning point for Hunter in more ways than he imagines. This could be the very thing that opens the door to his past and allows those buried memories to return—memories that are best left forgotten," she said.

"You know Hunter as well as I do. I'm sure he will be able to deal with it without going mad," Minerva said.

She was trying to convince herself more than she was Madame Laveau.

"He's stronger than anyone thinks—even himself," she added.

"Even so, I think we need to perform a small ceremony for him. One to give him the inner strength to deal with what he may learn. Would you care to join me?" Madam Laveau offered.

"I would be honored to," Minerva said.

"Then let us begin…." Madame Laveau said as she stepped to the altar.

Early the next morning, Hunter, Lorena and DuCassal stopped by the station to tell Valmonde what was going on. The Inspector looked up at them and shook his head.

"I don't like this one bit. What happens if you lose?" he asked.

"We don't intend to," Hunter replied.

"But just in case you do, what happens? How do we deal with this Baron after you're gone?" Valmonde asked.

"I'm not sure. That never crossed my mind," Hunter said. "You might have to make some sort of pact with him. Kind of like the one you have with Lorena and Hannah. Let him prey on the criminals as much as he likes and extract a promise from him not to feed on the general population."

"Can I trust him?" Valmonde asked.

"You can trust him as far as you can throw him," Hunter said. "Another alternative is to write to the Vatican and ask the Cardinal to send out more Slayers."

"I'd rather do that. Makin' a deal with the Baron is like makin' a deal with the Devil himself," Valmonde said.

"Worse," Hunter said. "At least the Devil keeps his bargains."

"When we defeat him, we'll come by and tell you all about it," DuCassal promised.

"What if you lose?" Valmonde asked again.

"Then you can gather up what remains of us in Washington Square," Lorena said.

When they left the station, DuCassal seemed more than a little quiet. Hunter noticed it and asked what was on his mind.

"Our coming battle," he said. "Can we defeat him, mon ami?"

"Damn straight we can," Hunter said.

"Definitely," Lorena agreed.

"But we'll need some sort of coordinated attack plan. We'll also have to use every weapon we have in our arsenal and add a few new tricks," Hunter said.

DuCassal nodded.

That night, Hunter and DuCassal began preparing for the fight by loading bullets and shotgun shells with sulfuric acid and holy water. They also added a few high explosive rounds to the mix, and the new shuriken Hunter had purchased. Both Minerva and Paul had given them bottles of blessed oil and Lorena sharpened the edge of her Bowie knife.

"Should we make a Molotov cocktail or two?" asked DuCassal.

"No. We don't want to set the park on fire," Hunter said.

"Or cause any more destruction to the general neighborhood than we have to," Lorena added. "I think what we have here should do the trick."

"And if not?" asked DuCassal.

"In that case, I suggest that you practice kissing your ass good-bye," Hunter said with a grin.

Later that evening, Tony LaFleur dropped by and offered to join the battle with them.

"I appreciate your offer, Tony, but I'd rather that you keep yourself in reserve—just in case we don't make it out alive. You're the only one left who understands what you'll be going up against if we fail. And you have the resources to get the job done," Hunter said.

"That makes sense. You don't want to put all your eggs into one basket," Tony agreed. "At least let me buy you dinner. Stop by the Dragon when you're finished. As usual, everything's on me."

"Thanks, Tony. We'll do that," Hunter accepted.

Hannah Morii was preparing for the battle in her own way. She spent part of the night leaping from rooftop to rooftop then onto the street. Each time she jumped, she drew her katana and brought it down with both hands as if she were slashing through something. Hunter had told about the Baron. She knew he was tough and fast. Her timing had to be absolutely perfect.

She also knew that no matter what happened, Hunter had to deliver the final, killing stroke. He had to write an end to the Baron's book by personally closing the last chapter.

Even Lorena wanted it that way.

Right now, the Baron didn't know about Hannah or Alejandro. Hunter wanted to keep it that way until the last moment. Hannah had no idea when Alejandro would decide to make his appearance. She just knew that it would be highly dramatic. There was more than little ham in Alejandro's "sandwich".

Alejandro spent his time drinking and trying on various opera masks in order to produce the perfect dramatic effect. After several bourbons and more than a dozen masks, he decided to stay with his usual attire.

"After all, it's always worked before," he reasoned.

CHAPTER TEN:
I Only Have Eyes For You

Savannah.

Four nights passed without even the slightest trace of fog. Carmello and Riccardo made their nightly patrols through the city streets and enjoyed meals at some of Savannah's finest restaurants.

Of course the O'Hara girls accompanied them when they went out to dinner or anywhere else other than the nightly patrols. Their father chuckled whenever he saw them together. He knew that a double wedding was in the near future—even if the Slayers didn't realize it yet.

By now, the locals were very familiar with them. Several even stopped to engage them in length conversations about this, that and the other. Everyone always greeted them with cheerful good morning/evening or just plain Hi ya'lls.

With very little effort on their part, the brothers had made an almost seamless transition into Savannah society.

The only person who didn't like them was Elise Toomey. She either snubbed them or "greeted" them with venomous glares. She also wished they would leave the city and the sooner they did, the better.

Her attitude made her a "person of interest" to the Slayers. She was the only one in Savannah who didn't seem to care about the killings.

In fact, Elise didn't seem to care about Savannah at all.

On the fifth night, the brothers were walking down Abercorn near Colonial Park Cemetery when the fog began to roll in. They stepped out to the middle of the street and watched as the locals quickly headed indoors to avoid becoming the next victim of the Wild Huntsman and his pack.

As the fog slowly obscured everything around them, Carmello turned to his brother.

"I'll remain in the open and act as the bait. You find yourself a good spot to shoot from. Whatever you do, don't miss," he said.

By then, the city landscape had once again changed into a bleak, barren wasteland. As Riccardo went to find a good vantage point, Carmello drew his revolver and waited. Soon, a ram's horn resounded through the fog. This was quickly accompanied by a series of loud howls and barks as the pack prepared to zero in on its prey.

"He's here," Carmello said as he checked the chamber of his revolver.

Riccardo had set himself up less than 100 feet away from his brother. He placed the stock against his cheek and peered through the scope. He could see everything clearly, even through the dense fog.

"Brother Parker does excellent work," he said with a smile.

They heard the horn sound again.

This time, it was closer.

Carmello watched as the pack emerged from the fog one at a time and began to circle him slowly. A couple recognized him from their earlier encounter and growled menacingly at him.

The rest just continued to circle.

The two closest ones made him wary. He knew one of them would try to attack first and, if Riccardo's shot didn't bring him down, the entire pack would be on him before he could take a step.

The largest wolf was a few feet to his left.

Another about 20 feet to his right.

The rest of the pack kept their distance as they waited for their leaders to make the first move.

Riccardo raised his rifle and took careful aim at the wolf to Carmello's right. He took a deep breath, exhaled slowly and squeezed the trigger. The report echoed through the fog like a thunderbolt.

A split second later, the bullet struck the wolf.

The impact caused the animal to jump nearly ten feet in the air. It fell to the ground right in front of Carmello and lay very still.

The rest of the pack turned and trained their red eyes on Riccardo, who quickly reloaded his rifle. Before the wolves could attack him, the ram's horn sounded through the fog once again. The pack howled, then turned and vanished along with the fog.

Riccardo raced over to his brother who was busily using his knife to extract the dead wolf's eyeballs. He had to take pains not to damage either of them, so this took several minutes. By the time he'd removed them, the wasteland was gone and the city of Savannah had reappeared.

Carmello put the eyes into a jar he had brought with him and twisted the lid tight. He held it up and smiled.

"We've got the eyes," he said cheerfully.

"All we need now is something personal from his last victim. Something she always has with her," Riccardo said. "Any idea what that could be?"

"We'll figure that out when we get to the morgue," Carmello said.

When they reached the morgue, the night watchman let them in.

"Do you still have the last girl who was murdered in the vault?" Carmello asked.

"We sure do. Why?" the watchman asked.

"We need something from the body. It's very important," Riccardo explained.

The watchman scratched his head and nodded.

"The mayor said we should give you boys whatever you need," he said as he led them into the far back room.

There were 100 metal vaults in the room.

"Most of these ain't occupied right now," the watchman said as he led them to a middle drawer and opened it.

"Here she is. I fixed her up as best as I could but she still ain't too pretty," he said as he pulled back the sheet.

"Thanks," Carmello said as they looked down at the mangled body.

"Now, what would be so personal as to be with her all the time?" Riccardo wondered.

"I've got it! Hair!" Carmello said. "That's personal and it goes wherever you go. It has to be hair."

Riccardo pulled out his knife and cut two inches of hair from the top of her head. He slipped this into his pocket.

"It'll have to do. If it's not what Anna wants, we'll have to come back," he said.

They slid the drawer back into the wall and locked the door. The night watchman saw them out and waited until they were out of sight before he returned to his nap.

A half hour later, they were back at the voodoo shop. They handed the jar with the eyes in it and the lock of hair to Anna. She took them and looked up at Carmello.

"Now I need something from you," she said.

"What?" he asked.

"Hair will do nicely," she said as she handed Riccardo scissors.

Carmello removed his hat and winced as his brother cut some hair from the back of head. He handed it to Anna.

She smiled and nodded.

"Follow me to the back. I need you to witness everything so you know it ain't fake," she said.

The back room was bare save for a series of shelves that contained jars of powders, bottles, candles and statuettes of various saints and deities. There was a small altar against the east wall with a statue of the Virgin Mary and another of Baron Samete on it. Directly above it was a wooden cross decorated with a ring of magnolias.

They watched quietly as Anna took the locks of hair and carefully wrapped them in a bright red cloth. She placed this on the altar and sprinkled it with oil and cloves. This done, she lit a red candle, said an incantation over the cloth and lit it. When the flames were high and bright, she took the eyeballs from the jar and carefully added them to the fire.

"In the name of Baron Samete, I command you to show me the face of the one who called forth the Huntsman! Let me see it now!" she shouted.

A few seconds later, a cloud of smoke swirled above the altar. Within it, a human face slowly took form The brothers stared as the image of a hawk-faced, dark haired middle aged woman appeared in the smoke.

"That's Mrs. Toomey! That's the mayor's wife!" Riccardo shouted.

"Why would *she* summon the Wild Huntsman? What's in it for her?" Carmello asked.

"Let's go and ask her right now," Riccardo said.

They hurried over to city hall and went up to the mayor's office. As usual, he was seated behind his desk doing some paperwork.

He stopped and smiled when they entered.

"What ya'll find out?" he asked.

"We found out who summoned the Wild Huntsman, but we have no idea why," Carmello replied.

At that point, Toomey's wife Elise burst into the office without knocking as always. Sheriff O'Hara was right behind her.

Elise sneered at the O'Sheas.

"I thought you'd left," she said icily.

"You'd like us to, wouldn't you?" Riccardo said.

"They just came over to tell me who's behind this monster that's killing half the city," Toomey said.

Carmello noticed that Elise blanched visibly when he said that and smiled. Now, he had no doubt she was behind it.

"You said you know who's behind this?" Toomey asked.

"We sure do and there's no doubt about it," Carmello said.

"Then who did it?" asked O'Hara.

Carmello pointed at Elise.

"Her! She's the one who summoned the Huntsman!" he said.

Elise stared at him.

"Elise?" Toomey asked.

"There's no doubting it, Mayor," Riccardo said. "She somehow managed to bring the Huntsman into our world, but for what reasons, only she can say. Your wife is directly responsible for deaths of 95 innocent people."

Elise pulled a dagger from her skirt pocket and charged at Carmello. He simply decked her with a right cross. When she hit the floor, O'Hara stepped on her hand until she let go of the knife, then picked it up and handed it to Carmello.

Then he not-so-gently dragged Elise to her feet and handcuffed her. She cursed and struggled the entire time, but he eventually forced her to sit down in one of the high-backed leather chairs.

"Miserable foreigners! You ruined everything!" Elise almost spat the words as she glared at the Slayers.

"That's what we get paid to do," Riccardo said smugly.

Toomey stared at her in disbelief.

"You summoned that thing? What on Earth possessed you to do that?" he asked.

"Those women!" she hissed.

"What women?" asked Toomey.

"The ones in the Savannah Ladies Poker Club!" Elise shouted.

"What? I thought they were your friends. You've known them all your life. Why would you want to get any of them killed?" Toomey asked.

"Those snooty, stuck-up women always hated me. Ever since we went to school together, they always made fun of me and treated me mean. I always swore I'd get even with them some day," Elise said. "So when I found that old book on magic spells and such in the store, I bought it just to see if something inside would be of use to me. And it was."

"What book? Where is it?" asked Toomey.

"It's right under your nose where you'd never notice it. You never notice anything! All you care about is this filthy city and its stupid, snobbish people!" Elise said.

"It's hard to believe that you've lived here all your life," Toomey said. "I never knew you hated this city so much."

"It's boring and hot and humid and filled with gnats and thunderstorms! When I married you, I thought you'd take me away from here. But you didn't! This is all *your* fault. You drove me to this!" Elise screamed with hate in her eyes.

O'Hara went over to the bookshelf and perused the titles. After a few seconds, he pulled an old, leather bound volume from the middle shelf. It was titled: Ancient Nordic Legends and Magic.

"Here's the book," O'Hara said. "She even bent the pages back on the spell she used."

Toomey leafed through it and shook his head. He tossed the book into a trash can.

"I'll have Floyd the janitor burn it so nobody else can get their hands on it. That book's caused us enough problems," he said.

"That book told me all about the Wild Huntsman and how to summon him. I brought him to kill all those women who were so mean to me when I was younger. And *he did,*" Elise said. "They're *all* dead now! Every single one! They'll never talk behind my back again!"

"Unfortunately, your lust for revenge also led to the deaths of several dozen, completely innocent people. The Wild Huntsman's on a killing rampage that will depopulate Savannah in a few years," Riccardo said.

"You're a bigger monster than he ever could be. You're responsible for the worst mass murder in Savannah's history," Carmello added.

"You're a real nasty piece of work, Elise!" Toomey said in disgust.

"I didn't mean for it to go this far—but I don't know how to send him back," Elise said with no real trace of remorse. "Besides, most of those other people were jealous of me, so they *deserved* to die, too!"

Toomey winced.

"You are one heartless bitch, Elise! I always knew you were a bossy, mean-spirited snob, but I never once imagined you do anything like this," he said. "You're so sick with jealousy and hate that it took over your life. None of those women ever said a single bad thing about that I ever heard or became aware of. Those women worked hard to preserve Savannah and its history. They were the cream of our society. And *you* murdered them as sure as if you'd stabbed them yourself."

"I hope the Huntsman keeps killing until there's no one left alive in the entire city!" Elise said bitterly.

Toomey and O'Hara looked at Carmello.

"Just how do we get rid of that thing?" asked O'Hara.

"According to the old legends, you have to give the Huntsman the head of the one who summoned him. He's supposed to take the head with him to the other side and never return," Carmello said.

"You mean we have to give him Elise?" asked Toomey.

Carmello nodded.

"Well, her head, anyway," he said. "He has no need for the rest of her."

"I doubt he'd want it anyway," Toomey said.

"You once said I was the most desirable woman in all of Savannah," Elise pointed out.

"That was then. This is now. You are far from being desirable. The only thing I've desired for the last five years is for you to leave and never come back," Toomey said. "You're a real *bitch!*"

Elise struggled with the handcuffs and glared at him.

"How *dare* you call me such a thing!" she shouted.

"There's many things I'm going to call you, Elise. Bitch is the nicest of them," Toomey said with a smirk.

"What it comes down to, Mayor, is a choice between the people of Savannah and your wife. You have to decide which is more important to you," Riccardo said. "If she lives, the Huntsman will keep returning until there's no one left. If you give him her head, he'll leave forever."

Toomey looked at Elise and shook his head.

"To me, that's a no-brainer," he said. "The people of this fair city elected me to do what's right by them and they trust me to get it done. I choose Savannah."

Elise stared at him.

"You can't be serious! I'm your wife! We've been married for 35 years!" she shouted.

"And I have smiled and put up your rotten disposition and temper tantrums for all this time. Wife or not, you tried to destroy this city and that is something I cannot and will not condone," Toomey said sternly. "You know, I've always wanted to divorce you. This is much better."

He turned to the brothers.

"You men can do what you want with her. Just make that Huntsman go away," he said.

"You can't be serious!" Elise shouted again as she struggled to break her bonds.

"I assure you, my dear, that I am dead serious. You caused the deaths of 95 innocent people. I'd shoot you myself but I just don't have the heart for it. It would be like shooting my favorite hound dog," Toomey replied with a smile. "Only I'd really miss that dog!"

"Bastard!" she shouted.

Toomey laughed.

"These men gave me a choice between your sorry neck and Savannah. I have made that choice. Farewell, Elise. If there is a Hell, I hope you burn in it forever," he added.

"Do you want us to shoot her in here?" Carmello asked.

"Or wait until we get her home?" Riccardo added with a smirk.

"Take her out back and shoot her. I'd hate to have her blood ruin the carpet. It's too hard to get out," Toomey replied. "Besides, I really like that carpet."

Carmello grabbed Elise by the arms and dragged her out of the office. Riccardo and O'Hara followed them out onto the street. A few people watched as they took her behind the building.

"Where's a good spot, Sheriff?" Carmello asked.

"Put her up against that tree," O'Hara said as he pointed at the stately moss-covered oak in the middle of the garden.

Carmello dragged her over and pushed her against the trunk. Elise remained silent the entire time.

If she prayed, no one heard her.

Not even God.

Carmello drew his revolver and placed the barrel against her heart.

"It's easier this way," he said softly as he pulled the trigger.

They carried her limp form to a bench. O'Hara went to the stables and returned with a large ax, which he handed to Riccardo. At that point, the mayor walked over. He held out his hand.

"I'd like to do the honors, if you don't mind," he said.

Riccardo gave him the ax and stepped back to watch as Toomey, rather gleefully, decapitated Elise.

When he was finished, he smiled.

"I've always wanted to do that. Thanks for giving me the opportunity," he said as he handed the ax to Riccardo.

The Slayers shrugged, then laughed.

"We need a long stick or pole," Carmello said.

"Will this do?" asked O'Hara as he held up a mop handle.

"Perfect!" Carmello said as he took it from and sharpened one end of it with Elise's dagger.

When he was finished, he picked up her head and rammed the pole up into it through what remained of her neck.

"We are you taking it?" asked O'Hara.

"I think we'll put it up near Reynolds Square so the Huntsman can see it. With any luck, the fog will roll in again tonight and we can get this over with," Carmello replied.

O'Hara, Toomey—and several bystanders—watched as they marched down Bay Street with their grisly trophy. When they were out of sight, the mayor and sheriff went back up to the office. Toomey broke open a bottle of ten-year-old Scotch and poured it into two glassed that contained cubes of ice.

"I thought I'd celebrate my emancipation," he said with a grin. "Care to join me?"

O'Hara laughed.

"Don't mind if I do," he said.

They clinked their glasses and saluted each other.

"I think we made a fair trade. Elise for Savannah," Toomey said with a wide grin.

"I think you made the best darned trade in the history of Savannah," O'Hara agreed as he refilled their glasses.

When they reached the square, Carmello rammed the other end of the pole into the ground. They stepped back and looked up into Elise's open, dead eyes.

"She even looks mean in death," Riccardo observed.

"She sure does," Carmello agreed. "When we took this assignment, I never imagined it would lead to this. I guess she brought it down upon herself, but part of me wishes there could have been another way of doing this."

"Most likely, they would have hanged her for murder. We just made things easier for everyone concerned. At least the mayor's happy!" Riccardo said.

They laughed.

"It *is* cheaper than hiring a divorce attorney," Carmello said.

He walked over to nearby bench and sat down. Riccardo walked over and sat beside him.

"Now we wait," he said.

Two hours elapsed before the fog began to roll in and blanket the city. They stood up and watched as the shadows of the city's trees and buildings slowly gave way to visions of a bleak wasteland. A moment later, they heard the horn in the distance, followed by howls and loud barks.

"They're here," Riccardo said.

They watched as the wolves charged into the square and stopped suddenly to stare up at Elise's head. Then they sat down and waited for their master to arrive. They paid no attention at all to the Slayers.

They just sat and stared up at Elise's head.

A minute or two later, the Huntsman rode up. He looked at the head on the pike, then nodded to the brothers as he plucked it from the pole. He whirled his horse around as he stuffed the head into a sack at his side. Then he sounded the horn and galloped off with the wolves hot on his heels.

A second later, the fog was gone and the city reappeared around them. That's when they heard the applause and realized they had an audience. Hundreds of Savannahians had gathered in the square to witness the last ride of the Wild Huntsman and his pack.

"We did it, Brother," said Riccardo. "We got rid of the Huntsman."

"Mission accomplished," Carmello said as they walked out of the square to the cheers and applause of the people. They could still hear them cheering when they reached Bay Street and walked over to Factor's Walk to take the steps down to River Street and their hotel.

To their surprise, Elizabeth and Kate were waiting for them in the lobby.

"Hurry and change! We're going out to celebrate!" Kate said. "Our carriage is just down the street."

CHAPTER ELEVEN:
Showdown in Washington Square

New Orleans, midnight.

At the appointed hour, Hunter, Lorena and DuCassal walked through the gate of Washington Square and followed the main path past a bizarre bronze sculpture that resembled a tuba. When they came to the large double-trunked sago palm in the middle of the Square, they stopped and looked around.

The large, full moon above cast an almost ghostly light over the park. Off in the distance, they could hear the sounds of jazz and rock coming from the clubs on Frenchman Street and the laughter of people.

It was a typical Friday night in New Orleans.

A young couple, both of them half drunk, started to meander through the park. When they saw Hunter and the others, they stopped.

"I don't think you want to be here right now," Hunter warned.

They knew who they were.

The man nodded, put his arm around the woman's shoulders and guided her out of the park. He knew something was about to happen. Something he didn't want to get mixed up in.

A moment later, the tall, caped figure of the Baron emerged from the shadows. He stopped before them and bowed his head courteously.

"You are prompt. I like that in my victims," he said with a grin.

"I think *you're* the victim tonight, Baron," Hunter said. "Because you're not leaving here alive."

"Bold words. I hope you can back them up," the Baron said.

"We'll soon see, now won't we?" said DuCassal.

The Baron laughed.

"You have balls! I like that in an opponent," he said.

"Before we begin, I have a few questions for you," Hunter said as they began to spread out.

"Ask what you wish," the Baron replied.

"We've fought several times now. In any of our encounters, you could have killed either of us. Yet you let us live. Why?" Hunter asked.

"I let you live because it suited me. You are both very good at what you do. You eliminate many of my competitors. Fewer vampires at large means more stupid humans for me to feel upon," the Baron said.

"There must be something more to it than that," Hunter pushed.

"There is something else. You and I have a more *personal* connection. We go back together much further than you imagine," the Baron replied.

"How far?" asked Hunter.

"How far back do your dreams go?" the Baron asked.

Hunter got an image of a man with dark, brooding eyes looking out over a plane of dead and dying men impaled on tall poles. Above it rose the flaming numerals 1462. He blinked to clear the images from his mind.

The Baron grinned at him.

"I also enjoy our little encounters. They amuse me. I also admire your tenacity. Anyone else would have given up the chase long ago, but you two keep coming after me. It's almost as if you are obsessed with killing me," he said.

"We're obsessed with taking you out the world," Hunter assured him.

"And we won't rest until we do," Lorena added.

The Baron laughed.

He looked at DuCassal.

"What do you say to *that?*" he asked.

"I'm with them," DuCassal replied.

"Are you good enough to take me down?" the Baron asked.

"We shall see," DuCassal replied.

"The last time we fought, you nearly killed me. Instead, you let me go. Why?" asked Lorena.

"Why would any father slay his own daughter?" the Baron put to her.

"Daughter? You're crazy. You're not my father," she said.

"In a way, I am your father. It was *I* who made you what you are now. I who created you. In that sense, you are my daughter," the Baron said.

"In that case, it's time to sever family ties!" Lorena almost growled as she launched herself at him.

The Baron stepped forward and punched her right in the jaw. The force of the blow was so powerful that it sent her flying across the park and over the fence onto Dauphine Street. Lorena hit the ground hard and lay still to gather her senses.

The blow was faster and harder than she expected.

"That was some punch," she thought. "I forgot how strong he is."

Hunter drew both revolvers and fired shot after shot into the Baron's body. Each bullet was loaded with an explosive charge and sulfuric acid which sizzled as it penetrated the Baron's flesh.

As the Baron staggered backward to avoid the hail of bullets, DuCassal stepped up and emptied both barrels of his shotgun into his midsection. Before he could recover, DuCassal attempted to bury a stake in his heart.

The Baron grabbed his wrist and threw him into the sago palm. He hit the top fronds and fell on his back between the twin trunks.

"Ow!" he yelped.

The Baron laughed.

Hunter drew his katana and moved in closer. The Baron saw him and backhanded him. The blow spun Hunter completely around and left him feeling a little dizzy. Before he could recover, the Baron seized him by the throat and pinned him against the fence. At the same time, they made eye contact.

"If you would know the truth, look into my eyes," the Baron said. "If you dare!"

Hunter did—for a moment.

He saw visions of castles, hellish battles and heard the cries and shouts of thousands of tormented souls. He saw an armored warrior on a black horse leading men in chain mail against a vast army of men in turbans while a village burned in the background. The air around them hissed with arrows of all shapes and sizes and fiery missiles arced overhead. The mounted warrior cut down everyone who crossed swords with him and laughed maniacally as if he reveled in the bloodshed and carnage.

Again he saw the numerals 1462.

The numbers faded to show an armored man being carried from the field on his shield while the battle raged around him. The warrior was almost dead, but somehow he lived to keep fighting.

That warrior, he realized, was *him*.

The images changed again.

They swirled together in a kaleidoscope of horror and mayhem.

Now came the forest of impaled, screaming men.

Now came images of two young boys playing at war, followed by two men arguing over something.

The images changed quickly.

Too quickly for Hunter make any sense of them.

He struggled.

The Baron tightened his grip.

Hunter snapped out of his dream and delivered a sharp kick to the Baron's groin. The Baron released him and stepped back.

"I've wanted to do that for years," Hunter said. "This, too!"

He raised his fist and brought it down against the side of the Baron's head. The blow only made him laugh.

"You never could get the better of me. Some things never change," the Baron said.

"You did. You became a monster!" Hunter said.

"Be careful whom you call a monster. There is far more blood on *your* hands than there is on mine," the Baron said as they circled each other.

"I kill because I *have* to. You kill because you enjoy it," Hunter said. "This is where it ends, Baron! I'm taking you down!"

"Bold words! Let's see what you've got," the Baron challenged as he pounced on him.

They rolled around on the ground while exchanging several punches. The Baron was the first to get to his feet. When Hunter tried to rise, he kicked him in the face and sent him sprawling.

The Baron laughed as Hunter shook the blow off and rose to one knee. Then he stepped back as Hunter charged. This time, he sidestepped him and punched him the back of his neck. The punch sent Hunter face-first to the pavement.

"This is too easy. I grow weary of this game," the Baron said. "Maybe we'll pick this up another time?"

He turned only to find his way barred by a dapperly dressed man in a bizarre opera mask. The man was leaning on the gate and smoking a thin cigar.

The Baron scowled at him.

"Get out of my way," he said.

The man simply blew a smoke ring and smiled at him.

"I think not," he said calmly.

Irritated, the Baron reached for him. To his astonishment, the man seized his arm and threw him against a nearby tree with enough force to knock a few leaves off. The Baron shook it off and studied his new opponent.

"Just who in Hell are you?" he asked.

"I am your worst nightmare," the man replied as he threw off the hat, mask and cape and instantly transformed into the largest rougarou the Baron had ever seen.

"Bah! I eat your kind for lunch!" the Baron sneered as he charged at him.

"I am *not* so easy to digest," Alejandro said as he sidestepped the Baron, grabbed the scruff of his neck and drove him face-first into the pavement.

The Baron struggled to his feet.

"Let me help you," Alejandro said as he grabbed his wrist and hurled him against the fence.

The Baron struck it hard and bounced off. Alejandro caught him before he hit the ground, lifted him above his head and body slammed him. The Baron leaped to his feet and punched Alejandro several times. To his annoyance, the werewolf simply stared at him, then bared his teeth.

"You'll have to do much better than that! You hit like a girl!" Alejandro teased.

They exchanged several more blows to no avail, then broke off and stepped back to study each other. Alejandro wasn't even sweating and he actually seemed to enjoy their encounter.

"Enough!" the Baron said as he sprouted wings and attempted to fly away.

Alejandro pounced on his back, forced him to the ground and ripped one of the wings from his body.

The Baron cried out in pain and anger as he tossed Alejandro off. The two circled each other for a few seconds, then attacked. They were still exchanging blows when Hunter and Lorena reached them.

The Baron saw them and attempted to leave, but Alejandro seized him from behind and sank his teeth into his shoulder. The pain caused the Baron to howl in agony. He reached around, seized Alejandro by the head and hurled him some 20 feet away. Alejandro easily landed on his feet and laughed.

"This is much more fun that I expected it to be," he said as he moved closer.

"I'm glad you're enjoying this as much as I. Too bad I have to kill you. I'm starting to like you a little bit," the Baron said as he circled to Alejandro's right.

Then, unexpectedly, the Baron turned and darted from the park. They chased him to Marigny and Royal where the Baron found DuCassal waiting with his shotgun.

"I thought I'd gotten rid of you," he said.

"Not quite," DuCassal said as he fired both barrels.

The shells struck the baron in the chest and splattered him with acid. The Baron grabbed DuCassal by the front of his coat, whirled him around and hurled him down an alley. He struck the wall hard and landed in an open dumpster. As he tried to struggle free of the trash, the heavy lid closed and struck him in the top of his head.

The Baron laughed.

Hunter seized the moment. He drew his sword and plunged it into the Baron's back until the blade broke through his chest. The Baron whirled and backhanded him across the face.

The blow stung Hunter but he didn't go down.

The Baron reached around and pulled the sword from his body just as Lorena charged and plunged her Bowie knife into his chest. The baron responded with a vicious uppercut that sent Lorena tumbling down the street. He then pulled the knife from his chest and tossed it over his shoulder along with Hunter's katana.

"I expected something different from you. Instead, you come at me with the same old tired tricks. I thought you'd be a little more imaginative this time," he said with an air of contempt.

"Here's one I haven't tried," Hunter said as he delivered a hard knee to the Baron's groin.

The Baron backed up a few paces. The blow had caught him off guard but did little damage. He responded by delivering a kick of his own to Hunter's groin. Hunter literally saw stars as he fell to his knees.

The pain was terrific.

Intense.

He wondered if the Baron had actually shattered something..

The Baron laughed.

He turned to leave only to be tackled from behind by Alejandro who had decided to rejoin the battle. The two began exchanging blow after blow like prize fighters in the middle of ring.

Lorena regained her senses. She got up and charged toward the Baron. He spotted her from the corner of his eye and decided to take care of two birds with one stone. He seized Alejandro by the arm, whirled him around and hurled him into Lorena. The collision knocked them both unconscious.

Hunter rose to his feet. He took a half dozen shuriken from his pocket and hurled them at the Baron before he could get out of the way. The weapons struck him in several places and exploded, sending bits of flesh and clothing all over the alley. Visibly annoyed, the Baron attacked.

"More parlor tricks? I'm getting bored with you, Hunter! So bored that I've decided to finish you off!" he said.

"Talk! Talk! Talk! That's all you ever do. Shut up and fight!" Hunter replied.

Hunter met him in the middle of the street and they slugged it out toe-to-toe for several minutes. Both men were more than a little frustrated that neither of them went down. Hunter seemed to be getting the worst of the match. He was cut above his right eye and his face was covered with bruises. To give himself a breather, he pulled a wooden stake from his mantle and rammed it into the center of the Baron's face.

The Baron reeled backward.

As he grappled with the stake, Hunter again kicked him in the groin. This time, he went down.

Hunter took the opportunity to catch his breath. He watched as the Baron got to his feet and pulled the stake from his face. He sneered and threw it at him. Hunter ducked and the stake became embedded in the wall behind him.

That's when Hunter spotted a shadowy figure watching from the roof of the building directly behind the Baron.

From her vantage point, Hannah Morii watched as the Baron charged at Hunter and gripped him by the throat. Hunter responded by wrapping his hands around the Baron's throat. As both men tried to choke each other to death, Lorena staggered to her feet and walked toward them. She spotted Hunter's katana lying on the sidewalk and picked it up.

As he and the Baron exchanged punches, Hunter looked up at Hannah and nodded. She caught his signal and nodded back that she was ready.

Hunter took a step back, hauled off and delivered a kick to the Baron's chest that sent him staggering toward the building.

Hannah gripped her katana with both hands and launched herself from the roof. As she fell, she aimed the blade right at the Baron's shoulder and brought it down with all of the strength she could summon.

Distracted by Hunter, the Baron never saw it coming.

The blade struck him in the left shoulder just to the side of his neck. The force of Hannah's weight behind the fall caused the katana to cleave the Baron from shoulder to groin as easily as a hot knife goes through butter.

"No!" he shouted as both halves of his body struck the sidewalk and spewed blood, intestines, parts of his lungs and flesh all over the pavement.

Hannah landed on one knee with one hand on the hilt of her katana and the point buried in the ground.

"Yes!" she said in a tone that Hunter thought was more than a little demonic.

He also noticed that she had an almost sinister gleam in her dark eyes.

She got up and grinned at him. Then, to his surprise, she slowly licked the blood from the blade before returning the katana to its sheath.

She saw the look on his face and chuckled.

"Blood is blood," she said. "There's no sense wasting it."

The Baron glanced at her and laughed. Then he smiled at Hunter.

"She is much like *you* were," he said.

"What's *that* supposed to mean?" asked Hunter.

The Baron simply laughed.

As the Baron's halves twitched hideously, Lorena walked up and handed the katana to Hunter.

"Finish him," she said.

Hunter raised the sword above his head. The Baron looked up at him and laughed. The laugh irritated Hunter.

"Fuck you!" he said as he severed the Baron's head from the right half of his body.

It rolled out into the gutter and grinned up at him.

Hunter sheathed his katana.

He took a bottle of sacred oil from his mantle and poured it over both halves of the Baron's body. He then picked up the head, placed it on top of the two halves and poured another bottle of oil on it.

The Baron laughed.

"What's so funny?" asked Hunter. "You're finished."

"It took you long enough but at last you've succeeded in destroying me. I salute—and pity you at the same time," the Baron said.

"I don't need your pity," he said.

"Are you sure?" the Baron asked smugly.

Hunter crouched down next to him.

"Before I consign you to the fires of Hell, I need you to answer one last question for me," he said.

"Ask," the Baron said.

"Who made you?" Hunter asked.

The Baron laughed.

His laughter irritated Hunter.

"What's so funny? Answer my question. Who made you?" he demanded.

"If you would know the answer to your question, I bid you to look into a mirror," the Baron replied.

Hunter stared at him for a long time.

The Baron smiled.

Hunter stood and struck a match.

He looked down at the Baron.

"Say goodnight, Gracie!" he said as he ignited the oil.

The Baron's laughter filled the air and rose with the smoke. It finally died down several minutes later when nothing but a pile of smoldering ashes remained.

Lorena, Hannah and Alejandro gathered around.

Lorena hugged him.

"We did it, Hunter. We finally killed that bastard!" she said with a sense of relief. "The nightmare is ended."

"Only until the next one comes to take his place," Hunter said as the Baron's last words echoed through his mind.

He smiled at Hannah.

"Thanks. You arrived in the nick of time tonight. You really saved my hide," he said.

"It was a pleasure. I heard what he said. What does it mean?" Hannah asked.

"I'm almost afraid to think about it," Hunter admitted. "He said if I want to know who made him, I should look into a mirror."

"But that would mean that *you* made him! Is that even possible?" asked Alejandro as he slowly regained his human form.

He quickly realized that he was nearly naked and excused himself to return to the park and retrieve his clothes.

"We should celebrate. How about Pat O'Brien's?" he called over his shoulder. "Say in two hours?"

"We'll meet you there," Lorena said.

She looked up at Hunter and saw that he was disturbed.

She hooked her arm in his.

"Don't think about it, mon cher. He was probably lying. You know how treacherous he was," she said.

Hunter nodded.

"I guess the Baron wasn't invincible after all," he said as he looked down at the smoldering ashes. "No one is."

At that point, DuCassal came limping up the street. Hunter, Lorena and Hannah sniffed and winced when he came close.

"You smell terrible," Hunter said.

"Twenty minutes inside a dumpster will do that to a man. I see that you finally got rid of that monster," DuCassal said as he spit into the ashes. "Is it possible for him to come back from this?"

"I hope not," Hannah said.

"I'd hate to have to do this again," Lorena said.

"Me, too," echoed Hunter.

"How about I go home and take a good, hot shower?" DuCassal suggested.

"Please!" all three of them said at once.

He shrugged it off with a chuckle and continued.

"Afterward, we can all go out and celebrate," he said.

"We told Alejandro we'd meet him at Pat O'Brien's in two hours," Hunter said.

"Sounds perfect!" DuCassal agreed.

On their way back to the Garden District, they stopped by the Basin Street station. DuCassal excused himself to go home and shower so as "not to offend the sensitive noses of the entire police force" by going inside.

When Hunter and Lorena entered the office, Valmonde was standing at the counter pouring himself a cup of coffee. He looked them over as he returned to his chair and sat down.

"You two look like you've been through a thresher," he commented.

"You should see the other guy," Hunter said as she sat down. Valmonde laughed.

"Since you're both here, I guess you beat him," he said.

"We did—with a little help from our friends. The Baron's nothing but a pile of ashes and a scorch mark now. We're headed home to get cleaned up. Afterward, we're going out to celebrate. Care to join us?" Hunter invited.

"Where you goin'?" Valmonde asked.

"We're starting at Pat O'Brien's. After we close it down, we'll head over to Brennan's for brunch," Hunter said.

"I would be delighted to join you to celebrate this auspicious occasion," Valmonde replied.

"Good. See you in a couple of hours, Chief," Hunter said.

Valmonde nodded and watched them limp out. He'd never seen either of them in such a tattered condition.

He looked up at Sam who had just entered.

"They sure look bad," Sam said.

"That they do. They'll both look fine by tomorrow—but there ain't no tomorrow for the Baron," Valmonde said.

The celebration lasted until late that afternoon.

By the time it was over, neither Hunter, DuCassal nor Valmonde were feeling any pain. When they left Brennan's, Hunter and DuCassal staggered to St. Charles to catch the streetcar home with Lorena acting as their "guide" to keep them from wandering aimlessly.

Valmonde and Alejandro walked Hannah back to her shop. Hannah invited Alejandro inside for a "daycap" while Valmonde hailed a carriage and told the driver to take him home so he could sleep it off.

For Lorena, it was if a great weight had been lifted from her shoulders. Her nightmare was over.

For Hunter, it was another matter entirely…

CHAPTER TWELVE:
Coda

Savannah, late afternoon.

Carmello and Riccardo rode over to the city hall. To their chagrin, a large crowd had gathered in front of the building. Most of them cheered and applauded when they arrived and dismounted. Mayor Toomey and Sheriff O'Hara greeted them at the front door with strong handshakes.

Kate and Elizabeth gave them big hugs and kisses.

"Don't they make cute couples, folks?" O'Hara asked.

The crowd cheered again.

Toomey raised his hands to quiet them, then made a speech praising the brothers for ridding their fair city of a terrible menace. He then asked his assistant who was standing behind him to give him the plaque. Toomey presented the plaque to the brothers and shook their hands while the people cheered and whistled.

Of course, the girls kissed them again, then hooked arms with them.

"What are your plans now?" asked O'Hara.

"Savannah is such a beautiful place and the people here are so wonderful, Riccardo and I have decided to stay—if you'll have us," Carmello said.

The crowd answered by cheering.

"Have you? Hell, we *insist* on that," Toomey said.

"But if ya'll are going to stay here, you might want to shorten those foreign-sounding names of yours. If ya'll make them easier to pronounce, folks here will warm up to you quicker," O'Hara said with a sly grin.

"Well, our father used to call me 'Mel' when I was younger. How's that sound?" asked Carmello.

"That's be just fine, wouldn't it folks?" said the mayor.

"*I* like it," Kate purred as she batted her eyes at him.

The crowd applauded.

"Mel" smiled and he tipped his hat.

"Then from now on, call me Mel," he said.

"I guess I could shorten my name to Rick," Riccardo suggested.

The crowd applauded again. "Rick" smiled and bowed his head.

"Rick sounds fine to me," Elizabeth assured him.

"Those names are fine. They make ya'll sound like you're from around here. But you'll have to work on those accents," O'Hara said.

"He's right. You boys do talk funny," Toomey joked.

"We like the way they talk, don't we Liz?" said Kate. "Ya'll sound so *exotic*."

"If ya'll are staying here, You'd best buy yourselves a house. In fact, I think I've got just the house for you," O'Hara said. "It's real old, like everything in Savannah. And it's fairly big."

"Is it haunted?" Mel asked.

"I'll say. Some folks believe it's the most haunted house in all of Savannah. And since ya'll are going to live here, ya'll know damned well you must have a ghost in your house. If you don't, folks will think you're kind of strange," O'Hara said.

"Or so low class that no self-respecting ghost wants to live with you," Kate added.

"Can you show it to us?" asked Rick.

"We can walk on over there right after the party," O'Hara said. "Right now, you're heading over to River Street. After all, you men are the guests of honor. Then I'll tell you everything I know about that house."

"Sounds good to me. How much will it cost?" asked Mel.

"You can get it real cheap because nobody's lived there for at least 20 years now—not since the last owner was murdered by whatever haunts it."

"Now you've really piqued my interest," Mel said.

"Mine, too," said Rick.

"Somehow, I figured I would," O'Hara said.

Back in New Orleans, things weren't going so well for Hunter.

The Baron's words kept echoing through his mind along with images of dark battles, victories against impossible odds and even an assassination attempt and betrayal.

Hunter tried to shake the images off by patrolling more often. And drinking more and more. On one occasion, he drank until he passed out, only to wake up screaming as the nightmares returned.

Days passed into nights which were interrupted by even more vivid nightmares. For ten straight nights, Hunter woke bathed in sweat and shaking. Only this time, he didn't take his usual walks. Instead, he got up and paced the floor while Lorena watched in silence.

She knew what he was going through.

She also knew why he didn't go out.

He was afraid of running into Madame Laveau.

Afraid of learning the truth.

Lorena was worried.

The man she loved was tormented by visions from his past. A past he buried centuries before. A past he wanted desperately to forget. But it kept coming back to haunt him in bits and pieces.

And those pieces were starting to come together whether he wanted them to or not.

Lorena just wished they would all go away and leave him in peace.

But the only way he'd ever truly find peace was to learn the truth about himself.

On the 11th evening, Hunter and Lorena were seated in the parlor. Lorena was reading the Times-Picayune for the latest crime news. Since Hannah had begun prowling the streets, the crime rate in New Orleans was dropping. Hannah, she realized, was averaging a kill per week.

That was far too frequent.

Vampires only needed to nourish themselves on human blood once per month. Hannah, she thought, was on some sort of rampage. Now that she had tasted human blood, she just couldn't seem to get enough of it.

"Perhaps her bloodlust will abate after a few more weeks?" she thought.

Right now, Hannah was feeling the power of being a vampire. For some, it was more than a little intoxicating. She hoped that Hannah would be able to bring it under control. She was also worried that she would one day have to take Hannah down if she got out of hand and began to feed on innocent people.

She looked at Hunter.

He'd been sitting with his head in his hands for over an hour. He hadn't spoken either. He didn't sleep much. He hardly ate. The Baron's last words were eating away at him like a cancer.

"If you would know the answer to that, I bid you to look into a mirror."

Lorena watched as he rose from the sofa and walked over to the large, ornate mirror on the wall near the front door. He stopped, blinked his eyes, and then stared into the antique glass.

Deeply.

As if were scrying.

Images of battles appeared, vanished and were replaced by another, more bizarre scene. This time, he saw someone grab another man by the throat and bury his fangs into his neck. As he let his victim fall to the floor, the vampire laughed.

"When you wake, you'll be cursed forever—just like I am. You will never know peace. Never know love. Never know death. That is my punishment to you for your betrayal, Georgi. It is a gift that will keep on giving until you grow weary of it and beg for death," the vampire said.

This scene was replaced by legions of impaled Turks set up like a grisly forest around a foreboding keep. There were thousands of tormented souls and their dying cries echoed through the valley.

Then came another scene.

This one was of a man in armor astride a coal black horse riding along the road that led to the keep. There were banners of dragons all around him and thousands of cheering soldiers.

Hunter continued to watch as the soldiers gathered around the man on the horse and banged their swords against their shields. Some raised and lowered spears, pole axes and banners. All were shouting over and over and over again.

That's when Hunter realized that they were shouting the warrior's name. And this time, he listened in horror.

"Dra-cu-la! Dra-cu-la! Dra-cu-la!"

"No!" he shouted as he struck the mirror with his fist and sent shards flying in all directions.

"No!"

Lorena rushed into the parlor and saw him standing amid the pieces of the mirror with a look that was somewhere between shock, sorrow and total disbelief.

"What did you see?" she asked.

"I—I saw *me*," he said.

He plopped down on the sofa and stared into space as he tried to sort everything out. Lorena sat beside him and leaned against his shoulder.

He put his arm around her.

"The dreams make sense now. They're all coming together in my mind. The battles. The flaming numerals. Everything. God help me," he said mostly to himself.

He rose and donned his hat and mantle. Then he looked at Lorena and smiled.

"I have to walk and think," he said. "Don't wait up."

He knew that she would probably follow him as she always did. When he left the house, she walked over and peered into what remained of the shattered mirror.

"What did you see, mon cher?" she asked.

Hunter headed straight for St. Ann. As soon as he hit the block where Marie Laveau's old house stood, a familiar mist began to swirl around him. He stopped in the middle of the block and waited. A moment later, Madame Laveau emerged from the mist and smiled at him.

"Good evening, Hunter. I heard about your battle with the Baron. You finally rid yourself of him. You should be smiling. Yet you look so depressed. Why?" she asked.

He took a deep breath, exhaled slowly and looked her in the eyes.

"I know who I am. You knew it, too. That's why you didn't tell me," Hunter said.

"Oh? And just *who* do you think you are?" Madame Laveau asked.

"I'm Vlad Tepis. I'm Dracula," Hunter said.

"No. You *were* the Impaler. You left him behind centuries ago, when you signed a certain contract," Madam Laveau said. "Remember?"

"Yes. I remember everything now. I made a pact with the Devil. He got what little remained of my soul. In return, he removed the curse I was under," Hunter said.

"He also granted you the gift of oblivion. He erased the memory of everything you did and agreed to allow you to continue to walk the Earth to rid mankind of the creatures that prey upon it for as long as you are needed. It was a most *unusual* contract. The first of its kind," she reminded him with a smile.

"I bartered my soul for a good cause. I wanted to make amends for the evil I had done," Hunter said.

"And you *have* many times over. You will continue to do so for as long as you are needed," Madame Laveau said.

"That could take an eternity," Hunter said.

"Immortality can in itself be a curse—if you allow it to be such," she said. "So far, I think you've handled it very well."

Hunter laughed.

Madame Laveau smiled at him.

This time, it was a gentle, almost soothing smile.

She touched his hand and he felt the burden leave his shoulders. For the first time in his life, he actually felt at peace.

"The man in your dreams is dead, Hunter. He will never return. A different and much better man took his place," she said.

"But I am both men," he said.

"No. The Impaler died the moment you signed that contract. He's gone forever. God has forgiven you a thousandfold for your past sins. It is time for you to forgive yourself," Madame Laveau said softly. "When you do that, the dreams will stop."

"You make it sound so easy," Hunter said.

"It's not easy. Only a very strong man can do what must be done. You, Hunter, *are* such a man," she assured him.

To his surprise, she kissed him on the lips. Her lips felt soft and warm and the kiss put him more at ease.

"Do you remember the first time we kissed? That was on St. John's Eve in 1800. That night, you literally swept me off my feet," she said.

"I remember," he said with a gentle smile. "We did have some good times back then."

Madame Laveau smiled.

"I'll see you around, Hunter," Madame Laveau said as she vanished along with the fog.

He turned to go back home.

Lorena stepped from the shadows of nearby buildings and put her arms around him.

"Did you see her this time?" he asked.

"I saw—and heard—everything, mon cher," Lorena said softly.

"So did I, mon ami," said DuCassal as he emerged from a doorway. He grinned at Hunter and laughed.

"Dracula, huh?" he teased. "You don't look anything like your old paintings."

"No. Dracula is dead. My name's Hunter," Hunter replied.

"That simply won't do. You can't go wandering around the rest of your life with only one name. That's just too strange—even for you. You'll need to have two names like most everyone else. You don't want to be mistaken for some tired old rock star or minor celebrity, do you? Since I've always known you as Charles, why not call yourself Charles Hunter?" DuCassal suggested.

"That works for me. What do you think, Lorena?" Hunter asked.

"You can call yourself whatever you like, but you will always be just Hunter to me—and the man I love more than life itself," she replied.

He put his arms around her.

"I'd be lost without you—*both* of you," he said.

"We know," they both said at once.

"How about Pat O'Brien's? I'm buying," DuCassal suggested.

"In that case, I'm drinking!" Hunter agreed.

"Me, too!" said Lorena.

En route to the restaurant, they cut through Jackson Square. To their surprise, Hunter led them to the steps of St. Louis Cathedral and knocked on the door. Several minutes later, a sleepy, half-drunk Father Paul opened the door and looked at them.

"Kind of late for a social call, isn't it?" he said as he led them inside. "What is it this time? Rougarou? Vampire or maybe a demon of some sort?"

"Something far more dangerous. I hope you're up to it," Hunter said.

"Well, what is it then?" Paul asked.

Hunter took Lorena's hand and looked into her eyes.

"I want you to perform a marriage ceremony," he said.

Lorena threw her arms around his neck and they kissed for a long time. DuCassal threw his hat on the floor and laughed as he hugged them both. Paul walked up and tapped them on the shoulders.

"If you're through with the proposal, we'll begin the ceremony," he said. "Did you bring the ring?"

DuCassal reached into his pocket and produced a beautiful braided set of wedding bands.

Hunter squinted at him.

"I picked them up a few weeks ago in preparation for this occasion," he explained with a wink. "One never knows when a wedding might break out."

"In that case, you can be the best man," Hunter said.

"Of course. Who *else* could you possible choose?" DuCassal replied smugly. "And she is much prettier than your first wife."

"You were married before?" Lorena asked.

"Yes," Hunter admitted as the memories flooded back into him.

"Anyone we know?" she asked.

"Marie Laveau," DuCassal said. "They were divorced five years later."

"That figures!" Lorena said. "Any children?"

"Just one—a daughter. We named her Marie, too," Hunter replied. "Madame Laveau kept her surname so that became our daughter's surname as well."

"My! You're just filled with surprises, aren't you?" Lorena said as they linked arms. "Any more coming up?"

"We'll see," Hunter said.

A few days later, Hunter's usual brief report reached the Vatican. Fra Capella brought it to the Cardinal's attention while he was eating breakfast at his desk. The Cardinal stopped eating to read it.

"I got by with a little help from my friends. Baron Georgi Konstantino Vlastrada is no more---H.

P.S.—Lorena and I are married."

The last sentence brought a wide grin to the Cardinal's face. He always knew it would happen one day. It just added another layer to their ever-growing, ironic mystique. It was another enhancement to their legend.

He also wondered if Hunter had learned anything about his long-obscured past? If so, just how much did he learn and how would such knowledge affect him? He also wondered if Hunter would ever let him in on that little secret?

He smiled.

Maybe such things are best left hidden.

"Even one such as Hunter can find true love. I now truly believe there is hope for us all. Maybe now, he will be at peace with himself," the Cardinal said.

Capella wrinkled his nose at the comment.

"But isn't she a *vampire*, Excellency?" he asked.

"Yes. And being such, she is the perfect mate for Hunter. Send them a card with my best wishes and send and additional $100,000 as a wedding present. They have earned that much at least," the Cardinal instructed.

"I'll do so at once, Excellency," Capella said. "We also received a report from the O'Sheas in Savannah. It's in their file which I placed on your desk. You'll need time to read it as it's quite detailed. To sum it up in Carmello's words: mission accomplished. They also wrote something about remaining in Savannah in order to ring a couple of southern belles—whatever *that* means!"

"Excellent! Then all is right with the world—at least for the moment," the Cardinal said with a smile.